The Teacher

AMISH COUNTRY BRIDES

Jennifer Spredemann

© 2021

Published in Indiana by *Blessed Publishing*.

www.jenniferspredemann.com

All Scripture quotations are taken from the *King James Version* of the *Holy Bible*.

Cover design by *iCreate Designs* ©

ISBN: 978-1-940492-57-5
10 9 8 7 6 5 4 3 2 1

Get a FREE short story as my thank you gift to you when you sign up for my newsletter here: www.jenniferspredemann.com

AMISH COUNTRY BRIDES

The Trespasser (Amish Country Brides)
The Heartbreaker (Amish Country Brides)
The Charmer (Amish Country Brides)
The Drifter (Amish Country Brides)
The Giver (Amish Country Brides Christmas)
The Teacher (Amish Country Brides)

NOVELETTES

Cindy's Story – An Amish Fairly Tale Novelette 1
Rosabelle's Story – An Amish Fairly Tale Novelette 2

OTHER

Love Impossible
Unlikely Santa
Unlikely Sweethearts
*An Unexpected Christmas Gift (Amish Christmas
Miracles Collection)*

COMING 2021 (Lord Willing)

The Widower (Amish Country Brides) book 7
Title TBD
Title TBD (Christmas book)

BOOKS by J.E.B. SPREDEMANN
AMISH GIRLS SERIES

Unofficial Glossary
of Pennsylvania Dutch Words

Ach – Oh
Aldi – Girlfriend
Appeditlich - Delicious
Bann – Shunning
Boppli/Bopplin – Baby/Babies
Bruder/Brieder – Brother/Brothers
Daed/Dat – Dad
Dawdi – Grandfather
Denki – Thanks
Der Herr – The Lord
Dummkopp – Dummy
Englischer – A non-Amish person
Fraa – Wife
G'may – Members of an Amish fellowship
Gott – God
Gut – Good
Hochmut – Pride
Jah – Yes
Kapp – Amish head covering
Kinner – Children
Kumm – Come

Maed/Maedel – Girls/Girl

Mamm – Mom

Ordnung – Rules of the Amish community

Rumspringa – Running around period for Amish youth

Schatzi – Sweetheart

Schweschder(n) – Sister(s)

Wunderbaar – Wonderful

Author's Note

The Amish/Mennonite people and their communities differ one from another. There are, in fact, no two Amish communities exactly alike. It is this premise on which this book is written. I have taken cautious steps to assure the authenticity of Amish practices and customs. Old Order Amish and New Order Amish may be portrayed in this work of fiction and may differ from some communities. Although the book may be set in a certain locality, the practices featured in the book may not necessarily reflect that particular district's beliefs or culture. This book is purely fictional and built around a fictional community, even though you may see similarities to real-life people, practices, and occurrences.

We, as *Englischers*, can learn a lot from the Plain People and their simple way of life. Their hard work, close-knit family life, and concern for others are to be applauded. As the Lord wills, may this special culture continue to be respected and remain so for many centuries to come, and may the light of God's salvation reach their hearts.

ONE

Martha Miller yanked on the reins of Quibble's harness, bringing the buggy horse to an abrupt halt beside the roadside mailbox.

"Stay here this time!" she warned the often unruly equine as she scurried from the carriage. "I'll not chase after you again today."

The horse nickered in protest, a response that typically meant he'd do whatever he pleased.

"Whatever. But *Dat* will be the one dealing with you." She threatened over her shoulder on her way to the mailbox.

A quick perusal inside the hollow metal box told her that the mail had already been snatched out by one of her siblings, or they hadn't received any today. The first scenario was the more likely of the two.

Quibble began fidgeting just as Martha hopped back into the buggy. "Oh, no you don't!" She cinched the reins, then gently loosened her hold on them. "Now, you march *nicely* toward the barn."

The horse took a few tentative steps, then shot down the driveway as though his tail had caught fire. Martha lost hold of the reins and would have flipped head-over-heels if there hadn't been a small backrest on the buggy's seat.

"Quibble! *Ach*! *Nee*." She managed to locate the renegade leather straps, wrapping them tightly around her hands this time. "You unruly creature. I'm sure and certain you'll be the death of me."

As soon as the horse spotted *Dat* near the barn, he slowed his pace to a gentle trot, then moseyed on over to the hitching post. As though he'd been a *gut* boy all day. Did he really think *Dat* hadn't seen his shenanigans? Who knew what horses thought, anyhow? All Martha knew was that this horse was too smart for his own *gut*. The mischievous beast.

Dat chuckled as he approached. "Is he still giving you fits?"

"It's not funny, *Dat*! That creature is the most stubborn, the most unruly, the most...frustrating thing we've ever owned." She huffed.

"Seems like he's met his match."

Martha thrust a hand to her waist. "What are you saying, *Dat*?"

"*Ach, dochder*, don't go getting your dander up. I don't mean anything bad by it. It's *chust* that you tend to be a little spirited yourself at times."

Ach. "I am not!" *Am I?*

Dat held up his hand, his thumb and forefinger bending a half inch apart. "Maybe *chust* a tad bit."

She glanced at the uncooperative beast, not caring to dwell on the creature another second. "Will you put him up for me, please? I'm too upset with him right now." She began walking toward the house, then called over her shoulder. "And no treats for him today!"

If she didn't see that animal ever again, she wouldn't feel bad about it. There was no doubt in her mind Quibble would indeed be the death of her.

Martha stomped into the house. She hadn't meant to slam the door.

"Who put a bee in your bonnet, Mizzy Tizzy?"

Ach, her *bruder* Paul was visiting home. He never failed to tease her about one thing or another. She needed to change the subject. She didn't want to lend one more thought to that wretched animal. "Small Paul, what are you doing here?" She teased back.

He flexed his muscles and raised one eyebrow. "Small?"

Martha snorted, then pretended to punch his gut.

"Hardly." She knew the sarcasm in her voice had hit its mark when he looked down at his stomach, which had expanded quite a bit since he'd gotten married to Jenny.

He slid onto the bench at the dining table. "Now you're looking for a fight. I can't help it if *mei fraa's* cooking is *appeditlich*. It sure beats the mush you used to try to feed me."

"*Ach*, I see how it is. I get no respect, and no thanks for attempting to keep *mei bruder* alive." She shook her head. "Besides, I'm not a bad cook."

"Let's *chust* hope *Jaden Beachy* thinks like you do." He chuckled.

"What do *you* know of Jaden?"

He grinned from his perch at the dining room table and held up a letter—one that must've come in today's mail. "Emily says you two have been writing to each other since Timothy and Bailey's wedding, *ain't not*?"

She snatched the letter from his hand. "What Jaden and I do is nobody's business but ours."

"*Ach*, so there *is* something going on between the two of you! *Gut. Mei alt maedel schweschder* needs rescued from her lonely life of misery."

She deposited her lunch box on the counter, then swatted his arm. "I teach scholars every day. My life is seldom lonely or miserable."

4

He clenched his heart dramatically, his voice changing to that of a narrator. "That's what she tells herself on those sleepless nights when she's dreaming of her knight in shining armor."

She snorted again. She didn't realize how much she'd missed having her ornery *bruder* at home. "Well, you'll win no fancy awards for that performance, I assure you."

"*Gut* thing for me that I'm only performing for an audience of one. And I *know* she's impressed." He took a bow. "Thank you very much."

Martha shook her head. "You're impossible."

"Impossibly charming is what Jenny says."

She rolled her eyes, taking a seat across the table from her older brother. "Impossibly annoying is more like it. I don't know how she puts up with you."

"She adores me. What can I say?"

"Why are you here? For real."

"So my younger *schweschder* can revel in the honor of my presence, of course."

"Seriously? That's what you came up with?"

"*Dat* wanted me to shoe the horses." He shrugged.

"It's nice to know you're *gut* for something other than spewing corny jokes."

"You wound me, *schweschder*." Paul clenched his heart. "But really. What *is* going on with you and Jaden Beachy?"

"We're friends. Pen pals."

"That's it?"

She sighed. "Yes, that's it."

"That's boring." Paul frowned.

"I don't think so. I enjoy writing letters."

"I thought there was something going on between you two."

She shrugged. "We live too far away. And I don't know...he's..."

"He's what?"

"I guess he's just not interested in me."

"That's baloney. Did he say that?" Paul shook his head. "Because *everybody* could see that he was definitely interested in you at the wedding."

Hadn't she thought so too? "I guess he must've changed his mind then."

"That doesn't even make any sense."

Martha laughed. "Since when do men make sense?"

"What did you write to him? Did you scare him off?"

She leaned against the chair's back, lightly tapping her school books. "I don't know. I don't think so. I mean, he's still writing to me. That says something, ain't not?"

"Do you think he already has a *schatzi* in Pennsylvania?"

"He said there was no *maedel*."

"Someone needs to whack that guy upside the head, I think. He can't see what's right before his eyes."

"He's free to stay a bachelor if he wants to. There's no law that says you have to get hitched."

Paul scratched his head. "But *why* wouldn't he *want* to? Marrying Jenny was one of the best things I've ever done. And he's not getting any younger."

"I don't know, *bruder*."

"Maybe I should call him up and have a talk with him."

"Don't you dare! You'd probably just make things worse."

"Well, he's already *not* courting you. What have you got to lose?"

"Like I said. We're friends. I'd like to at least *stay* friends. I don't think he has many."

"Why wouldn't he have friends?"

Martha shrugged. "I don't know. He seems like he's probably a little shy. I'm not sure. I mean, aside from the wedding, I haven't spent any time with him."

"He seemed friendly enough to me."

"*Jah*. But did you notice how he gravitated toward the folks he knew? He didn't really go out of his way to meet new folks."

7

"I think the only person he really wanted to spend time with was *you*, Martha. You two seemed inseparable."

A smile tugged at her lips, thinking of Jaden. He was such a sweet man, just like she'd remembered from their days as scholars. "I enjoy his company."

"*Jah*, well, too bad he doesn't live closer. Maybe he'd court you if you two could actually spend time together."

Ach, that would be a dream for sure and certain! But she wouldn't share her private thoughts with her *bruder*. "Well, he doesn't. So that's that."

"It doesn't have to be. If you just told him how you feel—"

She shook her head. "*Nee*. That's something I won't do. Besides, I'm quite certain he already knows. I wasn't exactly hiding my attraction. The ball's in his court."

"*Jah*, and that's where it will stay unless *you* do something about it."

"Paul, you know that's not my place. Besides, *Der Herr's* timing is perfect, ain't not?"

"I reckon."

"Well"—She stood from the table and lifted the stack of books into her arms—"I don't know about you, but I can't sit around and chat all day. I have papers to grade."

"Ugh. I'm so glad I'm not in school anymore."

She laughed. "And I'm glad you're not one of my scholars."

"Thanks." His tipped his coffee mug up and coaxed out the last of its contents, allowing the few remaining amber beads to drop onto his tongue.

She was sure and certain her *bruder* would never fully grow up. "You and Timmy Stoltzfoos were the worst in school."

"*Jah*, but I think we both turned out okay."

"That's debatable." She teased.

"I can hardly believe he's married to Bailey now." He sighed. "They sure do grow up fast."

"Paul, you ready to shoe your *schweschder's* horse?" *Dat* called from the doorway.

"Be right there, *Dat*." He dropped his mug onto the wash counter. "Well, duty calls, little *schweschder*." He tweaked Martha's cheek then followed their father out the door.

Jaden Beachy meandered out to the phone shanty, a practice he'd followed each night after supper for many years now. Most days, there was maybe one message, some days none, and other times several. He wondered what today's result would be.

He inspected the booth before stepping inside, and left the door open. Spring was catapulting toward summer at an alarming rate, it seemed, so their small phone booth was likely a sauna—or would be soon. Hopefully, there'd be no wasps inside this time. He'd cleaned out a nest last week and had been stung several times. Ugh, he hated wasps. He often wondered why they had to exist. But like many questions in his life, it remained unanswered. Oh well, it had been something interesting to include in his letter to Martha Miller, anyhow.

The light blinked on the answering machine. Some nearby districts had updated their landlines to cellular phones, but not theirs. Their leaders held tightly to the old ways, and change had always been slow in coming, especially where technology was concerned.

He really didn't mind so much, but in the last decade he'd gotten bored with life. It seemed like the same thing year in and year out. But more exciting things had been happening lately. First, his brother Josiah had turned back to the Amish fold, settled down, and finally married in Indiana. Then, his niece Bailey had gotten hitched just prior to last Christmas. And that was where he'd reconnected with his childhood friend Martha Miller.

He mused on her now. She was still like he

remembered—pretty, full of spunk, and not afraid to speak her mind on things. Unlike himself. *Nee*, he'd always leaned toward the shy quieter side. Not that he was afraid to speak his mind, he just usually didn't. He always figured that if someone wanted his opinion, they'd ask for it.

He'd once heard it said that every introvert needed an extroverted friend and vice versa. They also said that opposites attract. And he and Martha were opposite in a lot of ways. Yet, they had enough in common so that they got along well.

He recalled the first time she'd caught his eye. All the scholars had been sledding down the hill behind the school after the bell let them out for the day. He'd forgotten his sled and Martha had offered to let him use the one she'd brought to school. Her older *bruder* Paul hadn't known about the arrangement and had snatched the sled just as she was about to hand it off to Jaden. Her brother sped down the hill before Martha had a chance to stop him. Oh, but when Paul returned to the top, she was sure to give him a piece of her mind.

Jaden laughed, thinking of the moment now. He'd always admired her from that point on.

Then the world as he knew it had come crashing down.

He shook his head, not willing his mind to go in that direction. *Nee*, he'd been down that path too many times to relive it again.

He sighed, then refocused on his goal.

He pressed the answering machine's Play button, posed to jot notes on the notepad they kept on the shanty's small table. The first message had been about a dental appointment for one of his parents. And then the second one played. "Hey, Jaden, this is Josiah. I have a proposition for you. Will you call me back when you get the message, please? Thanks. Oh, and I'll swing by the shanty around eight tonight."

A proposition? What on earth did his *bruder* mean by that?

He wasn't sure what time it was, but he was certain it wasn't eight yet. He'd have to come back in a couple of hours. He picked up the phone and called back. "Hey, Josiah, it's Jaden. Just in case you get this beforehand, I'll try to call you at eight."

TWO

Martha scampered up the stairs to her room, then promptly shut the door behind her. She deposited her school materials on her desk. Correcting papers would have to wait. Jaden's letter took precedence.

After fluffing up her pillow against her headboard, she sank onto her bed. She stared down at the letter in her hands. *Gott, if it's Your will for me and Jaden to get together as more than friends, please pave the way for us. Honestly, Paul was right. I am lonely. I'm trying to be content, really I am. But seeing Jaden again seemed to spark that longing inside me—the longing for a family of my own. Of course, You know what's best. But if there's any way...* Martha let her silent prayer trail off into nothing.

She heaved a sigh, then slipped her letter opener underneath the envelope's sealed flap. The thought of

Jaden moistening the glue sparked a smile. She always sealed her envelopes with a secret kiss that no one but she and *Der Herr* knew about.

She grasped the precious contents from within and the letter fell open in front of her.

Greetings, Martha!
I hope this letter finds you well in body and spirit. I can't really say the same for myself, unfortunately. You see, I was attacked by wasps while trying to clean out their nest from the phone shanty. And yes, it was every bit as terrible as you can imagine.

Martha stopped reading. "*Ach*, poor Jaden!"

I have recovered somewhat, but the monsters definitely left their marks. It is something I never wish to encounter again. It's good that I'm not allergic to them, otherwise I would have had to take a trip to the hospital. Thank God, it did not come to that! Mom had some drawing ointment and it seemed to help within the hour. I should probably apply more, now that I'm thinking about it.

Other than that episode, I've had a pretty

decent week. Dad and I checked the fields today and the corn is coming up nicely. We should have a good harvest this year. Last year the corn was wonderful sweet. I wish you could have tasted it. I'm sure your sister Emily would like to sell some at her roadside vegetable stand that you mentioned in one of your earlier letters. It would be a good seller too, I assure you.

How are your scholars doing with their studies? I suppose the school year will be coming to a close soon. Do you have any plans for summer? How is your quilt coming along? Hopefully, you'll get some extra time to finish it once you're out of school. I wish I could see what your quilt looks like. I'm sure it's real nice.

Well, I guess I should close for now. Looking forward to hearing your goings-on!

With Care,

Jaden Beachy

Martha reread the letter, then folded it up and stuck it into her letter box. She still felt bad about the wasps. How terrible! Hopefully, now that it had been a couple of days, his stings had healed.

"Martha! Are you going to help with supper or not?" Emily's voice rang up the stairs.

Ach, had her sister already called her? "I'm coming," Martha grumbled.

Jaden's reply would have to wait for a more suitable time, when annoying little sisters weren't demanding her attention.

Jaden dialed the number to Josiah's phone shanty. He'd been sure to leave the house ten minutes earlier than necessary, so he wouldn't be late. Playing phone tag was the worst.

"Hello? Josiah speaking."

"Hey, *bruder*."

"Jaden!" He could hear Josiah's smile over the phone. "Just the man I wanted to talk to."

"What's going on?"

"We're doing good here. How's everything there?"

Ach, he didn't have in mind to chit chat. He'd been bouncing on his toes since hearing his brother's message, wondering what his "proposition" entailed. But he wouldn't be rude, that wasn't in his nature. "*Gut*. Everything is *gut* here. You said you want to ask me something?"

"I certainly do. Here's the deal. How do you feel about teaching?"

His eyes widened. "Teaching? You mean, like scholars?"

"That's exactly what I mean. I know you've only substituted before, but I also know that you enjoy books and learning, and you're pretty smart."

"I just filled in for a little while when the regular teacher was in the hospital." He frowned. "I guess I've never really considered it as a permanent thing. Why?"

"Our teacher is leaving. She's getting married this wedding season and we'll be in need of a new teacher. For whatever reason, they were wanting a man to take her place. Probably because they wouldn't leave to raise *kinner* is why, now that I think about it. Someone more permanent. You automatically popped into my head."

Ach, he'd be so close to Martha. And they'd have even more in common.

"How do you feel about moving to Indiana? You could stay with my family until you find a place of your own. Property is a lot more affordable here than in Pennsylvania."

He swallowed, pondering the idea.

"You there?" His *bruder's* voice echoed. "What do you think?"

"*Ach*, it's a lot to consider. Will it pay as much as my job at the lumberyard?"

"I'm not sure, but I can get more details for you. Since it would be permanent and you'd be the main bread winner for your family, when you have one, I think there's a pretty good chance they're going to pay you a fair wage. They might just ask you how much you need to be paid."

"I'd have to talk to *Dat*, of course."

"Yes, of course. But you're interested? I kind of spoke up first at the meeting, so you may have the first shot at the job."

"When do they need to know by?"

"Well, as soon as possible, I reckon. Probably before meeting this week will be *gut*."

"I see. Let me talk to *Dat* and I'll call you back tomorrow sometime."

"How about we just do eight tomorrow evening? It'll give you time to think about it. Of course, you wouldn't begin teaching until the next school year starts, which won't be till September. But I'm sure you'll need to go through training and such. I'll try to find out when the regional meeting is too."

"*Jah*, okay. But just wait. I'm not one hundred percent certain yet."

"Just be sure to pray on it too."

"I will, for sure and certain." Not that *Der Herr* would answer back.

"Do you have any questions?"

He pressed his lips together. "Not at the moment.

But I'm sure to have hundreds later."

"Well, if they come to your mind, just jot them down and you can ask me next time we talk."

"Sounds *gut*."

"Hey, Jaden?"

"*Jah*?"

"Between you and me, I don't think there's anyone more perfect for this job. You'd be great at it. You're kind. You're patient. You're smart."

"*Ach*, you are going to make me *hochmut*!"

"I'm just stating the truth, *bruder*."

"*Denki* for your words. But whatever *gut* I have comes from *Der Herr*." He deflected. If there was one thing he didn't care for, it was praise.

"I forgot humble." Josiah chuckled. "Anyhow, I'll be waiting for your call tomorrow."

"Sure." Jaden finally set the receiver down when he was sure and certain Josiah had hung up. Neither of them were much for long goodbyes.

Jaden blew out a breath, still stunned at Josiah's news. A teacher? *Ach*, it was an occupation he'd never considered before. Not that he thought it wouldn't suit him. He enjoyed the time he had briefly substituted. He liked *kinner* and learning. It would certainly be an interesting change of pace for him.

What did he really have to lose by accepting? He'd

be moving out from *Mamm* and *Dat's* place. How would they feel about it? Would they be pleased or would they discourage him? Or would they be indifferent? Whatever the case, the news would likely be as much a shock to *Mamm* and *Dat* as it had been to him.

It would certainly be an adventure moving somewhere he'd never lived before. He'd been in the same Amish district since birth, so adapting to a new *Ordnung* would take some getting used to, no doubt. He'd enjoyed staying at his *bruder's haus* when he visited for his niece's wedding and for Christmas. *Ach*, he'd had such a *wunderbaar* time!

The best part about accepting this proposal, though, would certainly be living close to Martha Miller.

THREE

Martha finally pushed her school papers aside and pulled Jaden's letter out of her special box. Now that supper was finished, the dishes were done, and her grading was complete, she could focus her attention on more exciting things.

She quietly reread the letter, then began her reply.

Hello, Jaden!

Ach, I was so upset to hear about your trouble with wasps! I do not envy you. I have only been stung by a bee and that was enough. I'm certain wasps stings are much worse. Anyhow, I hope you're feeling better now.

My brother Paul was here earlier, teasing as usual. I kind of miss having the older brothers at home sometimes, but I realize they have their families now. I wonder how long it will be before the others are off? I suppose only God knows.

My younger sister and brother, Susan and Nathaniel, are going on a mission trip this summer to Central America. They are really excited about it. A few others from our district will be going, as well as some other Amish up north. There will be a whole busload of them!

I've never gone on a trip such as this, but I hope to one day, if the Lord wills. Right now, I'm too busy with everything that I have to get ready for the scholars. I hope to tidy up and redecorate the schoolhouse. It is in need of paint and can use a fresh sprucing up. That will likely keep me busy, although I think there could be a frolic planned to help with the bigger projects.

What about you? Have you been on one of the mission trips? Or does your Ordnung not allow it? I think Silas mentioned something about it one time when we were talking about your brother Josiah's district. I don't think they allow it either.

My, your corn sounds delicious! I'd love to get my hands on some. As for my quilt, it is sadly at a standstill. I do hope to finish it this summer, but with Susan and Nathaniel leaving, that will mean extra work for the rest of us at home. We'll see how it goes.

Looking forward to your next letter!

Always a friend,

Martha

She folded the stationary and slipped the letter into the envelope. She'd send it off tomorrow.

Jaden hadn't meant to let the screen door slam behind him, but it seemed inevitable in his haste to share his news with his folks. *Ach*, he'd practically jogged back from the phone shanty.

"What has you all fired up tonight?" His father peeked over the top of *The Budget*.

"*Mamm, Dat*, I have something I'd like to speak with you about." He took a seat next to his father in the living room.

Mamm set her crochet project to the side. "Does this have to do with your *bruder's* phone call?"

"*Jah*, for sure it does." He rubbed his hands together.

Dat folded his newspaper and set it on his lap. "Well, out with it then."

He blew out a breath. "Josiah wants me to move to Indiana."

Both of his parents looked at each other and frowned. "Is this what you want?" his father asked.

"I should have explained first. Their district will be in need of a new teacher next school year and Josiah recommended me." He smiled.

"But you've never been a real teacher." His

mother's hands folded in her lap. He knew her words weren't meant to be condescending, so he chose not to accept them as such.

"Well, I did substitute for a while. Remember? Josiah said he thought I'd make a *gut* teacher, and they're looking for a man to take the job instead of another *maedel*."

"And you want to do this—become a teacher for *gut*?"

"I don't know, *Dat*. I'm thinking on it."

"Where would you live?" *Dat* asked.

"With Josiah and his family, for now. He said property is much cheaper out there. I do have some money saved up from my job at the lumberyard." He stared at both of them. "So, what do you think?"

"It's quite sudden," his mother said. "But if it's something you're interested in doing..."

"You are your own man now. It is a decision you'll need to make." His father shrugged. "How do you feel about teaching?"

"That's just the thing. Before today, I had never considered it permanently."

"You've always been a bookworm," his mother chimed.

"I'm thinking it just might suit me." He scratched the stubble on his chin.

"Would you still raise a crop, then?"

"I'm not sure. I could just have a large garden when I get a place of my own. I wouldn't need much. Josiah thinks they will pay decent since it would be my full-time job as head of the household."

"We would definitely miss you here."

"I know. And I'd miss you too. But you'd have one more reason to visit Indiana more often." He raised his eyebrows twice in quick succession.

Dat nodded. "Wasn't there a *maedel* out in Indiana that you'd taken a liking to?"

"That's Martha, the one I've been writing to. She's Silas Miller's sister. She's actually a teacher too."

"Oh?" His *mamm's* eyes widened, then he caught a sparkle. "You two attended school together when you were *kinner*, ain't not?"

"We did. She's five years older than I am. We were friends back then too."

"And now?"

"I don't know, *Mamm*. I do like her. A lot. She's really nice." *And pretty*. He'd keep that part to himself. "But we're just friends."

"That doesn't mean you *have to* stay just friends. Five years isn't a big deal. They say women outlive men, so marrying an older woman isn't such a bad idea." His father smiled. "And if you're going to be

25

living close to each other…"

Marrying? He ignored that part. "It's not that close, really." Jaden shrugged. "About an hour by horse and buggy." *Jah*, he was clearly making excuses.

"That's what drivers are for." *Mamm* picked up her crochet project, but a smile played on her lips.

"If I didn't know any better, I'd think you two are trying to marry me off." He looked back and forth at both of them.

"It's about time, ain't not?" *Dat's* eyebrow quirked up. "You know your *mudder* and I were *chust* twenty when we got hitched. You've already passed twenty-five. I don't know what you're waiting for, *sohn*."

"I'm…" He pressed his lips together. It would be best just not to say anything, as he'd always done.

"You're what?"

"I guess I'm just not ready. I'm not looking to get married."

"Will you wait till you're an old man and can no longer have *kinner*?"

"I don't…I just…I'd rather not talk about this." He stood. It was time to remove himself from this conversation. He hadn't been expecting it to take a turn for the worse. "So, you're okay with me moving to Josiah's, then?"

"If that's what you wish to do." His father eyed

him curiously. "But if you are not interested in this *maedel*, it is probably best not to lead her on and give her false hope. She's not a spring chicken anymore."

Chicken? Ach. He didn't know how Martha would feel being compared to a fowl, but he caught his father's meaning. "*Jah.*" He nodded. "I'll be speaking with Josiah tomorrow, then."

FOUR

"I think I'm going to accept the position." Jaden stated into the phone's receiver.

"Really?" He could hear his *bruder's* smile through the phone. "That's great, Jaden. Excellent."

"So, what do you need from me?"

"Have you talked to your employer yet? They'll probably want at least a two-week notice."

"*Jah*. I called my boss after I talked to *Mamm* and *Dat*."

"And how'd that go?"

He scratched his head. "With my boss or *Mamm* and *Dat*?"

"Both."

"Fine. *Mamm* and *Dat* were surprised, at first. But I think they don't mind the idea, especially if it helps me find a *fraa*."

His *bruder* chuckled. "*Jah*, that's *Mamm* and *Dat* alright."

"I feel kind of bad, though, leaving *Dat* in a lurch with harvesting the corn and all."

"*Ach*, I'm sure he'll just have Justin and Joshua help, or he can hire someone. They'll adjust. I wouldn't worry about it."

"When do you think I should head out there, then?"

"Anytime is fine with me and Nora. I'm sure the leaders will want to meet you and all that. Of course, you probably won't be receiving a paycheck until you actually start school in September."

That was four months away yet. "Hey, I was going to ask. Martha had said something in her letter about a mission trip. Is that something your *g'may* participates in?"

Josiah chuckled. "Over the bishop's dead body."

"That bad, huh?"

"*Jah.*"

"But the two groups are allowed to mingle?"

His brother sighed. "For now. We'll see what happens."

"What do you mean?" Jaden frowned.

"They're pretty upset about the whole mission thing. I don't know what will happen if they decide we can't have fellowship with them. My daughter lives in Bontrager's district, for crying out loud. Not to mention Silas and his family."

And Martha.

"As you can tell, I'm a little frustrated."

Jaden rubbed his forehead. "I see."

"I *won't* be cut off from my daughter, that's all there is to it."

"What will you do?"

"I'm guessing if they do decide to break fellowship, there will be a split in our *g'may.*"

"How does Nora feel about all of it?"

"She's torn. This is where she was born and raised. Of course, Miriam and Michael are here too. Nora and Miriam are best friends. Then there's Nora's folks." He blew out a puff of air. "It's a mess."

"Yikes. So, you still think I should come?"

"Well, you've been forewarned. Nothing is set in stone yet. But if there does happen to be a split, there will likely be a need for *two* teachers. So no need to worry about job security." Josiah chuckled wryly.

"Well, that's something."

"So, do you have any idea of when you might come?"

"Could you ask the leadership when they'd like me there? Four months is a while to go without pay, so I'm thinking of sticking around here for a little bit. Unless if they want me there already. You said there would be a teachers' meeting?"

"*Jah*. I'll get all the details for you."

"Would you do me a favor, Josiah?"

"What's that?"

"Don't tell anyone about this. I'd like it to be a surprise for Martha."

"You really like her, don't you?"

"She's a *gut* friend."

"I see. Well, I can't promise anything because there are some who already know. But I'll try to keep it under wraps. It would be a *gut* surprise for the *kinner* too, now that I think about it. I'll mention it to Nora. We haven't said anything to Bailey or Silas, so we're good there."

"Okay. I'll try to get all my ducks in a row here."

"I'm looking forward to seeing you, Jaden."

"You too." The phone clicked off.

Now, to pen his letter to Martha.

⁓

Greetings, Martha!

I'm doing well. Thanks for your concern regarding the wasps. Fortunately, there is little evidence of their terror now. It is all just a bad memory. If I ever have to tackle that sort of thing again, I think I will borrow a full body suit from a beekeeper. I'm just glad it's over!

I hope you can still squeeze time into your summer schedule to work on your quilt. How long is the mission trip for? Is it all summer?

I admit that the mission thing sounds interesting. I've never considered such a thing. It isn't something our people usually do, so I'm a little surprised your district leaders are allowing it.

I understand about siblings leaving home. Seems like this house keeps getting emptier as my brothers and sisters marry off.

I can't really say anything yet, except that I have a surprise! I wish I could say more, but it'll have to wait until a later time.

I hope this letter finds you healthy and happy.

Your friend,

Jaden Beachy

Jaden sighed. He wished he could tell Martha all about his upcoming new venture, but he wanted it to be a surprise.

What would Martha think if he just showed up on her doorstep one day? He couldn't wait to find out!

FIVE

Martha packed her things into her messenger bag and said goodbye to the last student, before locking the schoolhouse door. She turned around, then nearly jumped out of her skin when Titus Troyer almost bumped into her.

The young widower was a first cousin to her best friend Amy. He'd always been of the timid sort. He seemed kind too, but maybe she just thought that because she'd never really talked to him much.

"I'm sorry." He apologized. "I didn't realize you'd be leaving so soon."

She glanced over his shoulder at his three children sitting in the buggy, her smile tentative. "Did you...need something?"

He removed his hat, twisting it awkwardly in his hands. "Uh, *jah*. I...I...uh...was wondering..."

She nodded slowly to encourage him to continue.

"Well, you know, since Helen passed on last year. You see, uh, I don't make a very *gut mamm*." He frowned, then shook his head. "*Ach*, this isn't coming out right. What I mean to say is would you consider...?"

Her lips twisted. *Ach*, she hoped he wasn't going to ask what she thought he might. "Consider...?"

"Becoming their *mamm*." The words rushed out. "You see, you're real *gut* with the *kinner* and they like you, and seeing as you're not hitched yet..." He shrugged. "I was thinking that I would ask anyhow."

Martha gasped. "I'm flattered, Titus. Really. And I do enjoy having your *dochder* in my class. But see, the thing is..." *Ach*, she shouldn't lie. But if there ever *could* be anything between her and Jaden, then she wanted to keep her options open.

"You're already courting someone, ain't not? *Ach*, I'm sorry. I hadn't realized..." He glanced toward his *kinner*.

"It's okay, Titus. I do hope you can find someone."

He nodded curtly, his face reddening slightly. "We'll go now. I'm...I'm sorry."

Should she say thanks for asking? *Nee*, she'd leave it at that. The situation was already awkward enough. *Oh boy. A marriage proposal?* She certainly hadn't been expecting *that* today!

He quickly turned and hasted to his awaiting buggy.

As Martha watched the family head down the road, she wondered what their life was like without a *mamm*. Did Titus know how to prepare meals and such? *Ach*, she couldn't imagine. Hopefully, he had someone to help him.

It was true that her heart went out to him, but she had no interest whatsoever in becoming the poor man's *fraa*.

Martha pulled into the Millers' Country Store and Bakery, owned by her oldest brother Silas and his *fraa* Kayla. Kayla and their sister-in-law Jenny, Paul's wife, mostly ran the store with help from Kayla's daughter Bailey Stoltzfoos and occasionally Martha's youngest sister Emily.

The moment Martha walked inside, she was reminded why this store had become a hotspot in their community. Jenny must've just taken a loaf of bread from the oven.

"What is that *appeditlich* smell?" She closed her eyes and inhaled.

"It's the pretzels," Bailey volunteered. "If you want one, you better grab one now before the rush comes in. We've already made two batches today and sold out of both of them."

"*Ach*, business must be *gut*." Martha perused the bakery case.

"*Jah*, it's been great. I don't know how *Mamm* and *Aenti* Jenny keep it running and still keep the *kinner* in one piece."

Jenny walked in from the back, carrying a little one in her arms. "Fortunately, I have helpers. And your *onkel* Paul has limited my hours away from the *haus*." She informed Bailey.

Jenny turned to Martha. "We have doughnuts left over from this morning, if you'd like to take them home to the family. *Gott* knows your *bruder* doesn't need them," she said. "I can bag them up for you, if you'd like to hold this one."

Martha stretched out her arms to receive her youngest nephew. "I'm sure they'll enjoy them." It seemed like every time she visited the store, she left with free leftover baked goods.

"Did you stop by for anything in particular?" Bailey asked.

"*Jah*, actually. I need thread." Jaden's comment in her letter had reminded her that she was out of a particular blue color. Hopefully they carried it here.

"It's in aisle two." Bailey pointed. "Do you need help?"

"*Nee*. I should be able to find it alright." The store was so tiny, it only had three aisles. But the items they carried were useful to most Plain folks. The bakery took up nearly half the store space, not counting the back area where the large ovens were.

Somehow, this little store felt like a slice of home. Perhaps it was because she was related to everyone who worked here.

"Where is that blue thread?" She whispered to the little one, stroking his fine hair. "*Ach*, here it is." She grasped two spools, then headed up to the counter. "I'll take a pretzel too," she told her niece.

"Sure." Bailey grabbed the tongs, took one of the large pretzels from the warming case, placed it on a foil sheet, grasped a napkin, then handed it to Martha.

"*Denki*." She smiled as she handed the *boppli* back to Jenny and took the bag of leftover baked goods.

She pulled off a steaming section of the pretzel and popped it into her mouth. She couldn't refrain from groaning. "So *gut*." Too bad Jaden wasn't here to enjoy one with her.

"I know, right?"

Sometimes Martha laughed when the loved ones around her used *Englisch* phrases, but she supposed it was only natural since Bailey's mother had grown up *Englisch*, and her Amish father had lived in the

Englisch world for almost two decades.

"Anything new?" Martha asked.

The corner of Jenny's mouth lifted as she glanced at Bailey, a hint of knowing dancing in her eyes.

"What?" Martha's gaze ping ponged between her niece and sister-in-law. "Don't tell me...Bailey..." She leaned close to her niece's ear. "Are you in the *familye* way?"

Bailey nodded, but her smile didn't quite reach her eyes.

Concern prickled on Martha's skin. She glanced at Jenny, a question in her mien. "What's wrong? Is everything okay with the *boppli*?"

"*Ach*, don't get her started," Jenny said, shaking her head.

Martha was confused now. "What do you mean?"

Jenny looked at Bailey. "Do you want me to tell her?"

Bailey nodded, her lips smashed together.

"She's had morning sickness and—"

"Timothy won't let me go on the mission trip now!" Bailey exploded. It looked like tears threatened to fall. "It doesn't matter what I say, it's 'No, I don't want anything to happen to you.' It's ridiculous! Timothy and I were the ones who got Jerry Bontrager and the leaders to even consider it. We're kind of in charge of our group. We can't *not* go!"

Ach.

"I'm sure he's just concerned for you and the *boppli*." Jenny assured.

"*Jah*, well, I could just as easily be injured in a buggy accident out on the road," Bailey said, swiping away a tear. "Timothy doesn't know how much this means to me."

"And *you* don't know how much you and our *boppli* mean to *me*." A masculine voice echoed behind Martha.

Martha turned around at the sound of Timothy's voice. *Uh-oh.*

"Bailey, it would kill me if something happened to you and our *boppli*. I'd never be able to forgive myself." He walked close to his wife and lowered his voice. "The conditions aren't desirable. You could get really sick from the water or by eating something foreign."

"But we'd be going there to help improve the conditions. Remember, we're installing those pumps so they'll have fresh running water to drink?"

Martha's gaze volleyed between the couple as they scuffled.

"Bailey, you'll be miserable traveling all that way. You could hardly come to work today." He shook his head. "If only you could have seen yourself."

"I'll take ginger."

Timothy's hands clenched. "Bailey, be reasonable."

"If we don't go this year, then tell me when we will go." Bailey frowned.

"There will be other opportunities, *fraa.*" He insisted.

"*Nee*, there won't. The *bopplin* will keep coming and our lives will just get busier. Don't you see? This is our *only* chance, Timothy! It's now or never." A cascade of tears fell against her cheeks. "Sometimes I think you don't even care about how I feel."

"I'm not against you, *schatzi*. I love you." Timothy's frown deepened, then he and Bailey seemed to realize that Martha and Jenny were still in the same room, hearing their every word.

Bailey hung up her apron on a peg on the back wall. "If you'll excuse us, *Aenti* Martha and *Aenti* Jenny, my husband and I will continue this discussion on our drive home." She nodded curtly, then rushed out the door.

Timothy followed quickly behind her. Before he left, though, he turned to them. "Am I wrong in wanting *mei fraa* and *boppli* safe?" He didn't wait for an answer. His shoulders sagged as he slugged out the door.

"*Ach*, the poor things." Jenny shook her head, jostling the *boppli* in her arms. "Marriage is tough sometimes."

"I can imagine." Martha looked around at the empty store. "Do you need help? Was Bailey supposed to leave early?"

"*Nee*, but her hours have been sporadic lately. I'm used to working by myself. There's only an hour left yet. I can handle it."

"What about the *boppli*?"

"He'll just go into his playpen back here. He's a real *gut boppli*, so he'll be fine."

"You're sure then?"

"*Jah*. Besides, Kayla's just down the driveway. If she sees that it's busy, she'll send Shiloh out to help."

That was one of the things she liked about the Amish ways. No one was ever alone, at least, not in their community. Martha smiled as she left with her abundance of baked goods.

Now, to coax Quibble into getting her home in one piece.

SIX

"There's a letter for you on your desk," *Mamm* said as Martha walked through the doorway. She glanced at Martha, attempting to suppress a smile. "It's from Jaden Beachy."

Ach, she supposed it was nearly impossible to have any type of a private life when your family knew all your goings-on. At least no one had witnessed the exchange between her and Titus Troyer. She decided that was something only her journal and *Der Herr* would be privy to. No one else needed to know.

"*Denki, Mamm.*" She glanced around the kitchen, attempting nonchalance. She set the baked goods on the table. "Do you need help with preparing supper?"

"Maybe later. You go read what Jaden has to say." *Mamm* shooed her toward the stairs. "I know you're anxious for his words."

So much for nonchalance.

Ever since the Stoltzfoos-Miller wedding, it seemed *everyone* expected her and Jaden to get hitched. But honestly, she didn't think Jaden was all that interested in her. *Jah*, they'd hit it off at the wedding. *Jah*, they were *gut* friends. *Jah*, they wrote letters to each other. Often. But that didn't mean that he was head-over-heels for her. He never indicated anything more than friendship, so why should she expect it? Why should she lay her heart out for it only to get trampled on? Why had she gone and fallen in love with Jaden Beachy?

Ugh.

While still in her mother's view, she took her time removing her bonnet and placing it on the mudroom counter. She patiently took her lunchbox to the kitchen and cleaned out its contents. When there was nothing left to do, she meandered up the staircase to her room.

Once inside, with the door closed, she sat at her desk and smiled down at Jaden's envelope. There wasn't anything different about it, except for the stamp, which had red hearts on it. *Nee*, she wouldn't read anything into it. It was just a stamp, after all. One that he likely got from his mother's stash. But just the same, it caused her heart to gallop.

She used her letter opener so as not to make a torn

mess of the thing, then pulled out his single-lined page. While she wanted to savor each word, that proved nearly impossible when receiving one of Jaden's letters. *Nee*, instead she devoured the thing and it was over all too quickly.

But this time...

This time his words lingered. *I have a surprise.*

Ach, for sure and certain it was going to drive her crazy not knowing what Jaden's surprise was all about. What a big tease. How could he expect her to be content with *I have a surprise*? Didn't he know a proclamation like that was akin to pure torture?

What on earth could it be? *Oh no. What if he...?* She didn't want her mind to go there, but it did. What if Jaden Beachy had met a young woman and had fallen in love with her? What if the surprise was that he was getting married? Would she be able to accept that and move on? *Ach,* she'd have to. She wouldn't have a choice.

Jah, that was probably the most likely thing. After all, people in their Pennsylvania district kept courtships hush hush until the wedding. And since they were *gut* friends, he had to share the news with somebody.

Gott, please don't let that be what it is. But if it is, please help my heart to be able to bear it.

Nevertheless, she'd write back to Jaden. If they were going to end their friendship, she supposed sooner was better rather than later. Especially if he had someone special. And he most likely did, given how excited his penned words seemed.

She sighed and pulled out her stationary. This very well could be one of the last letters she would send to Jaden Beachy. The thought made her sad. Melancholy, actually. This letter would be difficult to write, because she wasn't feeling it. But she would pretend to be happy for his sake.

Hello, Jaden.

I'm so glad you've healed up now. The bee suit is probably a good idea.

I just bought more thread for my quilt today, so maybe I'll get some stitching done on it.

Your surprise sounds interesting, but you know it's not nice to tease someone like that. All I can do is wonder what your surprise might be. Could you at least give me a hint?

Your friend,
Martha

It was short, but sufficient. And for now, while her emotions were doing somersaults, it was all she could muster. It would have to be good enough. She'd send it off tomorrow.

She thought on her day, now. The issue with Timothy and Bailey reminded her that marriage wasn't always a walk in the park or a lovely buggy ride. It came with its own set of problems. Perhaps she should just be content as she was.

Or maybe she should reconsider Titus Troyer's offer. What if he was her only chance at having a family of her own?

Jaden turned Martha's letter over in his hands. "That's it?" He mumbled the words to himself. She'd never written something so brief. Perhaps she'd been in a hurry. Or maybe she was just as excited as he was about his surprise and wanted to find out about it as soon as possible. There was only one thing to do.

He'd better write her back right away and give her a hint as to what it was.

Hello, Martha.
If you must know about the surprise, I can give you a hint. A big one.
Here is my surprise:

I GOT A NEW JOB! Or, at least, I'm getting one soon.

As you can tell, I'm pretty excited about it. I'm still not exactly sure when I will start my training for it, though.

Before long, you'll know ALL the details, but hopefully that is enough to satisfy your curiosity for now!

By the way, I was surprised that your letter was so short. Not much news to tell?

My brothers aren't too happy with my news because it means they'll have to help Dad out on the farm much more. But I think it will be good for them to learn more about farming and spend more time with Dad out in the field.

Fathers can teach valuable lessons even when you don't realize it. I've learned a lot from my father, and I look up to him greatly. He is a wonderful good example for us boys. I hope I can be like him someday, but I have a long ways to go.

Anyhow, I feel like I'm prattling on now. I look forward to your next letter. Hopefully, it'll be a little longer next time?

Your friend,

Jaden

SEVEN

Martha couldn't wipe the smile off her face.

A job? That was it?

Ach, she'd been foolish to jump to conclusions and let her thoughts run away with her. Jaden had even said he wished her letter had been *longer*! Did that mean he couldn't get enough of her words? *Ach,* it seemed so.

It was only a new job! So, she'd fretted over *nothing* for an entire week. Now she felt like a fool. But, fool or not, it was only a job!

Jah, she'd be on a cloud all week, of that she was certain. And she'd be sure to write Jaden a longer letter this time.

Jaden leaned back against the seat and settled in for the long ride to Indiana. He'd opted to hire a driver instead of taking the bus or a train. He preferred privacy over being in the public eye, even if it cost him a little extra money.

Being Amish already attracted enough attention from passersby. He wouldn't invite more. To some folks, his people were simply a novelty. Other folks were indifferent. And then there were some folks who were downright hostile. He'd never understand that. Why couldn't people just mind their own things and leave other folks alone? The world would be so much better if everyone would just follow the Golden Rule, as he'd been taught—do unto others as you'd want them to do unto you. It was a simple concept, to his thinking.

Nevertheless, he couldn't wait to get to his destination. They'd do most of the trip today, then stop in the evening to enjoy a meal and rest at a motel overnight. Then they'd be on their way again first thing in the morning. If his driver's calculations were correct, and if they left the motel when scheduled, he'd be at his *bruder's* house around ten in the morning. From there, he planned to eat, freshen up, and relax until late afternoon.

Hopefully, in the evening, he'd be able to visit Martha. If he hadn't feared word getting out about his arrival, he would have chosen to wait until the next day. But he wanted her to be surprised. *Ach*, he couldn't wait to see the look on her face.

Martha's thoughts had been preoccupied with Jaden again. Not a *gut* thing when one was in charge of putting supper on the table at a reasonable hour. Fortunately, she'd chosen something simple. She'd been craving tomato soup and grilled cheese sandwiches. It was the perfect thing since the rain over the last few days had brought milder temperatures.

She resisted the urge to peek into the oven at the coffee cake she'd made for dessert. It would be wonderful *gut* for an evening snack tonight. Everyone seemed to love her coffee cake, but she was quick to quell the pride that threatened to fill her heart.

A knock on the mudroom door drew her attention. From where she stood in the kitchen, she couldn't see who it might be.

"Martha, will you get that?" *Mamm* called from the top of the stairs. Where was everybody, anyhow?

"*Jah*, sure." She moved the pot of soup to the warming rack. The sandwiches had finished several minutes ago, but were keeping warm.

Just beyond the door stood an Amish man, but he was facing the opposite direction. She frowned, wiped her hands on her apron, then turned the doorknob.

And then he turned around.

Martha gasped. "Jaden?" Her hand immediately flew to her wayward hair and she tucked the unruly strands beneath her *kapp*. *Ach*, she must look a sight!

A smile stretched across Jaden's face. *Ach*, she'd nearly forgotten how handsome he was. "Surprise!"

"What are you...you're *here*!" She hated when she got all tongue tied.

"I hope it's okay that I stopped by unannounced. I wanted to surprise you."

She looked down at her dirty apron, then tugged her bottom lip between her teeth. His eyes collided with hers and locked momentarily. She cleared her throat, then let her gaze fall to the floor.

"You surprised me alright." She shook her head. "Would you like to come in?"

"I was hoping you'd like to go for a ride." He gestured to the horse and buggy behind him. "I borrowed it from your brother, Silas."

Ach, Silas knew Jaden was here?

Wait. Jaden wanted to take her on a buggy ride?

"Have you eaten yet? Supper just finished and I was about to call everyone to the table." She motioned toward the kitchen.

"As a matter of fact, I haven't." His smile broadened.

"Would you like to eat with us, then? I made plenty. It's nothing fancy, just grilled cheese sandwiches and tomato soup."

"I'd love to." He glanced to the horse that was tied to the hitching post. "Our ride can wait."

Perhaps he should have given Martha warning. She seemed a little out of sorts, but she looked lovely, to his thinking. Hopefully, the family wouldn't mind that he had shown up right before supper.

After they—Jaden, Martha, her folks, her brother Nathaniel, and sisters Susan and Emily—were seated around the table and the silent prayer had been uttered, he waited for one of the plates of sandwiches to be passed around. *Ach*, they smelled so *gut*! How long had it been since he'd indulged in a grilled cheese sandwich?

"So, Jaden, what brings you out this way?" Martha's father asked before dipping his sandwich into his soup.

"Martha, actually." He noticed that all eyes went straight to Martha and her cheeks blossomed with a becoming blush.

Ach, he hadn't meant to embarrass her. He hung his head. "Or, did you mean to Indiana?"

"*Jah*." Her father smiled.

"Well, I actually wanted to share that with Martha on our buggy ride after supper." He smiled. "I kind of wanted it to be a surprise."

"I see." Her father nodded.

"You're full of surprises today, it seems," Martha said, ignoring all eyes on her.

"How is your father's corn coming along?" Her father continued the subject. Thankfully, he hadn't asked about work.

"*Ach*, I almost forgot." His gaze shot to Martha. "I brought you some corn. It was from last year's harvest. My *mamm* kept it frozen. I have it in an icebox."

"*Ach*, your corn! I can't wait to taste it. I'll have to fix it up tomorrow." Martha's smile stretched across her face, causing her eyes to crinkle at the corners.

"I better go get it out of the buggy. It should probably stay frozen until it's cooked." He excused himself, hurried to the buggy, and grabbed the paper grocery bag. He stepped back into the kitchen and held the bag up. "Should I put this in your icebox?"

"*Nee*, I can do it." Martha's *mamm* volunteered. "*Denki* for this, Jaden. And for thinking of Martha."

He didn't miss the look Martha's *mamm* exchanged with her daughter. Clearly, she thought they were courting. *Ach*.

He realized he'd forgotten to answer her father's question. "The corn is coming up nicely. I see yours is too."

"*Jah*. Should have a nice harvest come September."

"I can't wait to taste it." Jaden grinned.

"You're planning to stay till September, then?"

Jaden nodded, ignoring the questions in everyone's eyes. "*Jah*. I'm sure you'll hear all about it after our buggy ride."

But for now, he needed to keep his words to himself and finish the delicious meal *Der Herr* and Martha had graciously provided for him.

EIGHT

The cool breeze felt *wunderbaar* on Martha's face after being in the hot kitchen most of the evening. She climbed into Jaden's, or Silas's, carriage. Was she really going on a buggy ride with Jaden Beachy? Surely, he wasn't courting her. *Nee*, they were just *gut* friends. That was all. He'd never expressed any romantic interest in her. Not really.

But she was sure and certain that her family had misconstrued his visit as a date, which it wasn't.

She slid her gaze in Jaden's direction as he held the reins. A smile played on his lips as though he harbored a delicious secret. Martha guessed that he was waiting until they were out on the road to speak his mind. Hopefully, it would be soon, because not knowing was driving her crazy.

"You're awfully quiet over there." Jaden flicked a glance in her direction.

"I'm patiently waiting. Or at least trying to." She laughed.

"I guess there's no time like the present." He grinned, turning onto the main road. "You know how I said I was getting a new job?"

"*Jah*?"

"Well, it's *here*. In Indiana."

"*Ach*, it is?" Her eyes widened. "Seriously? So, you're not just visiting. You're *moving* here?"

"That's right. To my *bruder's* Amish district. I'm staying with him until I find a place of my own."

"*Ach*, Jaden! That's *wunderbaar*!" She felt like hugging him, but she wouldn't, of course. It wouldn't be proper for friends.

"I thought so. But the bad news is that we probably won't be writing letters anymore. It might be kind of silly since we'll be so close."

"I wouldn't mind. But seeing each other in person is even better, ain't not?"

"It is, for sure."

"So, what job are you taking then? Have you started yet?"

"*Nee*, not yet. Remember I mentioned the training?"

"*Jah.*"

"Well, I was hoping *you* could maybe help a little with that."

Her lips twisted. "Me?"

"I'm taking over the school in my *bruder's* district. Their teacher is getting hitched and they wanted a male teacher who wouldn't leave once he settled down. Somebody permanent. Josiah suggested me to the leaders, since I'd substituted before for a short time. I'll meet with them, then with the parents who are on the school board, this week."

"*Ach*, you're going to be a teacher too? I can hardly believe it." Warmth filled her.

"Believe it. I'm here in the flesh, ain't not?" He chuckled.

"That, you are. But you need *my* help?"

"I do. Since I don't need to join the class until next week to see how things go on there, I hoped that I could join you this week. Maybe be your helper, see how you handle your classroom, and hopefully get some pointers."

"*Ach*, the *kinner* would love that. Especially if you play ball with them at recess."

"Really? *You* don't mind?" His smile grew.

"*Nee*. Not at all. It'll be fun having another adult in the classroom." She nudged him with her shoulder. "Maybe you can even help me grade papers afterward."

He nodded. "I can do that."

"Wow, you did have a big surprise!"

61

"Hopefully, a pleasant one." His brow arched.

"The most pleasant." That was when she finally noticed where they were going. "The schoolhouse?"

He pulled into the side yard. "You wouldn't happen to have your keys with you?"

"*Nee*, but I keep an extra one hidden." She winked.

He slid down and tied the horse to the hitching post.

"You'll have to keep your eyes closed while I get the key."

"Don't trust me, huh?"

"I do, but the schoolboard insisted that I tell no one where the spare is kept." She shrugged. "Sorry."

"I guess you gotta follow the rules." He closed his eyes, but his smile remained in place. "You're not going to disappear on me or anything, are you?"

"Well, that would be pretty rude of me, wouldn't it? You come all the way from Pennsylvania to see me, then I go missing."

"People would talk, for sure and certain."

She laughed. "People are already talking." She twisted the key in the lock. "You may open your eyes now."

"Thank you. I was starting to fall asleep."

"Standing up?" She chuckled.

"It was a long drive from Pennsylvania. We drove

most of yesterday. I'm not used to sitting that long. I'm feeling lazy."

She thought about his home in Pennsylvania. Since her family left their home state when she was quite a bit younger, she hadn't missed it all that much. But Jaden's situation was different. "I'm sure your folks are going to miss you."

She walked into the classroom and Jaden followed.

"*Ach*, I'll miss them too. It's pretty much my first real time away from them, and away from home."

"You'll adjust. It'll be weird at first because you don't know a lot of people in your *bruder's* district. But once you get to know people, you'll be more comfortable. Getting to know the *kinner* will help you connect with the parents. If the *kinner* like you, the parents will."

"Let's just hope they'll like me." He chuckled. He walked around the classroom, perusing the desks, the décor, the children's projects she'd stapled to the wall.

"I don't know anyone who wouldn't. You're a very kind person."

Jaden stopped all of a sudden, then stared at her.

"What?"

"I think that's the nicest thing anyone's ever said about me."

Her? Nice? She felt like snorting. But she couldn't

help but be kind in Jaden's presence. He had an aura about him that seemed to rub off on her. He truly brought out the best in her. "It's the truth."

"May I share something with you?"

"Of course. Anything."

"I think you're the best friend I've ever had."

"*Ach*, Jaden. You can't mean that."

"I most certainly do." He insisted.

"Well." She shrugged, not really knowing what to say. "*Denki*. I think of you as a really *gut* friend too."

"*Jah*." Jaden frowned, but turned away before Martha could field his expression. Was that what he wanted? What *she* wanted? Friendship? He'd thought so. But now that he was here with her, his feelings were becoming all *ferhoodled*. In his heart, he desired more than just a friendship with Martha. But his mind told him it could *never* be, no matter how much he wanted it.

Ach, maybe spending time with her wasn't such a *gut* idea after all.

Martha stood behind her desk looking very much like a teacher. "We typically start the day around eight thirty..."

She continued, but Jaden could no longer comprehend

her words. Thoughts roared in his head and seemed to drown out everything around him. He couldn't do this. He couldn't be here with her.

"Jaden? Did you hear me?" She snapped her fingers.

He blinked. "*Ach*, I'm sorry. What was...what did you say?"

"What's wrong, Jaden?" She came close. Too close.

He shook his head several times. "I don't think I should be here."

"Why not? What do you mean?"

"This. Me helping out here. It isn't a *gut* idea."

"Why?"

Ach, why did she have to look so pretty standing there? Why did she have to show such concern for him? Why did she have to smell like cinnamon and sugar? Or was it sugar and spice and everything nice?

"Because I might..." He couldn't stop his hand that lifted to her impossibly soft cheek, seemingly of its own accord. Neither could he stop the lowering of his head. Nor could he stop the touch of his lips to hers.

When Martha stepped into his embrace, time seemed to stand still. He tilted his head slightly and deepened the kiss at the touch of her fingers feathering through the hair at the nape of his neck. His hat slipped off and fell to the floor. He pulled her closer still, but he couldn't seem to get enough. If they stayed like this forever, it would end too soon.

A gush of wind from outside broke the spell, and he finally came to his senses. *Ach*, what on earth was he doing?

"Martha." He swallowed. "*Ach*, I'm sorry. I shouldn't have…"

He looked at her. Saw the longing in her eyes. Her love for him. And it all but killed him. Because he knew a real relationship between them could never work.

He turned and ran out of the schoolhouse.

"Jaden!" Martha's troubled voice hollered after him.

He ignored her and kept running. He needed to get away. Not from Martha, but from himself. Why had he made such a mess of things?

"Jaden, wait!" *Ach*, was Martha following him?

He hadn't wanted her to.

"Jaden! Stop. Please."

He could probably run for a couple of miles without stopping, but he wouldn't force Martha to follow after him, which is what it looked like she intended to do.

He stopped, then turned around. "I don't want you to follow me."

"Too late. I'm here." She panted.

He was actually surprised either of them had that much energy after the kisses they'd shared.

"Why did you run away?" And that was one of the things he both liked and hated about Martha. She was bold and to the point and she spoke her mind.

"Martha, we can't do this. *I* can't do this."

"Why? Why, Jaden? What's wrong with me?" Tears shimmered in her eyes.

Ach, he hadn't wanted to hurt her. He hated seeing her tears, knowing he'd caused them.

"You?" He blinked. "Nothing is wrong with *you*. You are wonderful." He frowned. "It's what's wrong with me."

"What's wrong with you?"

"I'm no good for you. I'm no good for anyone. But especially you."

"Jaden, why do you say that? Why are you talking this way?"

Emotion welled up in his throat, clouded his eyes, but he suppressed the tears. "Because it's true."

"No, it's not."

"It is." He squeezed his eyes closed at the onslaught of tears.

"Tell me why."

"*Nee*. You wouldn't understand. Nobody would."

"Let me try. I want to help you."

"*Nee*. I can't be helped! I'm cursed, don't you see? I'm cursed for life!" He spun around and took off in a sprint back toward the schoolhouse. This time he wouldn't let her catch up to him. He would jot a quick note, then hide out until she left with her *bruder's* buggy.

Ach, this had all been a big mistake. A mistake he'd never be able to live down.

NINE

Martha sat on her bed, staring at the wall. A box of tissues was on one pillow and a bag of chocolates on the other. A pile of soiled tissues and empty wrappers lay in a heap in front of her.

How could such a *wunderbaar* evening have gone so wrong?

She closed her eyes, recalling every sensation she'd felt while she'd been in Jaden's arms. *Ach*, he was such a fantastic kisser. Of course, he was the only one she'd ever kissed, so she had no one to compare him to. But still. She couldn't imagine *any* kiss being better than that one.

But as wonderful as it was, it had ended in disaster.

She'd had fantasies about Jaden staying after their buggy ride and indulging in some of her coffee cake. She'd thought about the two of them sitting alone in the *schtupp*, after they'd spent time playing games with the rest of the family, and everyone else had gone to bed. She'd thought Jaden would tell everyone of his plans to teach and to help out at the school for a week, and she imagined *Dat* offering to let him use the *dawdi haus*, so he wouldn't have to hire a driver twice every day. She would have pretty much had him to herself for an entire week.

Instead, she'd returned home alone. She'd refused to speak with anyone, so she figured the family probably had guessed how it went. Most likely, they were all feeling sorry for her now, thinking she'd be destined for *alt maedel*-hood for the rest of her life.

At one time, she may have believed it too. But not now. Not after Jaden's kiss.

Now that she knew how Jaden felt about her, there was no way she was going to let him slip through her fingers. They loved each other, plain and simple, and no one was going to convince her otherwise.

Not even Jaden. She didn't know what he was going through, but she was determined to help him overcome it.

Love was enough to get one through anything, wasn't it?

She bowed her head. *Dear Gott, please help Jaden*

with whatever he's going through. Help him to see that You love him and that You can help him overcome anything. Denki. Amen.

He hated himself.

How could he have done that to sweet Martha—the best person he knew? He had to be the biggest *dummkopp* to ever walk the earth.

Why had he gone and ruined their friendship? What they'd had was precious. Now, it was non-existent. Because he knew in his heart she'd never think of him the same way again. He'd blown it.

A tap on the bedroom door stole his attention. "Wanna talk about it?" *Josiah.*

"*Nee.*"

"You haven't said a word since you got back. I think you need to work through this—whatever's bothering you." The closed door muffled his words, but Jaden got the gist of them.

"Just go away. Please."

"Jaden..." His brother's voice sounded laden, like his own heart. "Okay. But I'd like you to come with me tomorrow."

"Where?"

"Sammy's."

Jaden frowned. "Who's Sammy?"

"Sammy Eicher is Michael's *grossdawdi*. You remember my friend Michael, ain't not?"

"*Jah.*"

"Well, the guys get together every Saturday morning. We enjoy a time of fellowship, usually over coffee and breakfast. Sound good?"

Jaden groaned.

"Listen. You don't have to say a word while you're there. Trust me, there'll be plenty of talking without your needing to put in your two cents. You'll have a *gut* time."

"Fine." He sighed. "What time?"

"We'll leave here around six thirty."

"And I thought I was on vacation."

"No such thing, *bruder.*"

"So much for sleeping in," he mumbled.

"What was that?"

"Nothing. *Guten nacht.*"

"Good night, Jade."

"And who is this new fellow joining us today?" A spry older man, whom he guessed was Michael's *grossdawdi*, eyed Jaden.

"This"—Josiah's hand clamped his shoulder—"is

my younger *bruder*, Jaden."

Sammy stretched out his hand, a smile glistening in his eye. "*Gut* to meet you, Jaden."

He shook the older man's hand, already feeling at ease around him—something that wasn't typical for Jaden. "You too."

"I'm guessing you know everybody else?" Sammy asked.

"*Jah.*" But he wasn't sure if being around Martha's brothers was such a *gut* idea. What had Martha or her father or brother said when returning Silas's horse and buggy? Jaden had been the one to borrow it. He *should* have been the one to return it too. That would have been the responsible thing to do. Another failure on his part.

"We ready to start?" Paul rubbed his hands together.

"*Jah*, I'm starving." Jaden smiled.

Everybody seemed to stop what they were doing and turned to look at him. He looked at Josiah. "What?"

"You didn't tell him?" Michael said. "That's not nice."

"Tell me what?" Jaden's brow furrowed.

"Bible before breakfast." Sammy nodded. "That's how it goes in this home. Seek ye *first* the kingdom of God."

Jaden turned to Josiah, his brow raised.

"We have a Bible study first. But you can grab a cup of coffee. Breakfast will be in about a half hour."

Jaden's stomach chose that moment to grumble loudly.

Sammy chuckled. "Don't worry, *bu*. You won't starve to death."

"No you won't." Paul yawned and stretched wide. "I brought some of Jenny's cinnamon rolls."

"And I brought Kayla's quiche." Silas added.

"Quiche? I'm not sure I've tried that," Jaden said.

"*Ach*, you'll love it," Michael said. "It's kind of like a breakfast casserole in pie crust."

Jaden shrugged. "Sounds good." Of course, at this point in time almost anything would qualify as sufficient fodder.

"Time to start. Get your coffee, *buwe*, and mosey on over to the living room." Sammy directed.

"Timothy isn't coming today?" Paul looked at Silas.

"*Nee*, Bailey needs him," Silas said.

Josiah whispered in Jaden's ear as he poured his coffee. "She's in the *familye* way."

"Oh, wow. I hadn't realized..." Jaden supposed since Bailey and Timothy *had* been married several months now, it was certainly possible. He just couldn't get over seeing his niece as a little girl, even though he'd attended her wedding in December.

"They grow up fast." Silas locked eyes with Josiah and they both nodded.

"Don't I know it." Sammy shook his head. "At this rate, I'll be a *gross, gross, grossdawdi* before too long."

"Is there such a thing?" Jaden chuckled.

Michael sighed. "*Mei sohn* is nineteen, so there's a *gut* chance."

"*Jah*, well. Let's *chust* hope and pray he doesn't move as fast as his *vatter* did." Sammy eyed Michael.

"Right." Michael nodded.

Sammy sat in what looked like an ancient hickory rocker, while everyone else took whatever other seats were available. "Enough chit chat. Let's pray."

Jaden sat open-mouthed as each man gave his testimony. *Ach*, if *Der Herr* could forgive some of the stuff he'd heard about today, was it possible there was forgiveness for *him* as well?

They went on to read the testimonies of different men in the Bible, and how *Gott* delivered each one out of the bondage of sin.

Jaden's eyes burned. It couldn't be *that* simple, could it?

"So you see," Sammy said. "Their sins were no match for the grace of God. There is no sin He won't pardon, no transgression too wicked for our Lord's love to cover." He looked at each of them. "What a mighty, wonderful God we serve. Let's give Him thanks."

A half hour later, Sammy joined Jaden on the porch swing. The older man sipped on a fresh cup of coffee. "That breakfast sure was *gut*, ain't not?"

"*Ach*, you guys were right. It was wonderful," Jaden said.

"A *fraa* that can cook is a blessing from *Der Herr* indeed." Sammy nodded. "My Bertie was a blessing, for sure."

"How long has she been gone?"

"About seventeen years now. There isn't a day I don't still miss her. I reckon I'll be joining her in glory before too long."

"It must've been hard to lose someone that close to you." Jaden had never lost anyone close to him, though, for a time, he thought his *bruder* Josiah may have died. But when a body was never recovered, it was difficult to accept his death as a fact. Jaden hadn't known if it was intuition or what, but he'd always had a question in the back of his mind about his brother's disappearance all those years ago. So when he'd encountered him on the street one day, he hadn't been totally shocked. It had just been confirmation that what his heart had suspected was indeed true.

"*Der Herr* got me through it. Sent Michael's *fraa* Miriam to help me out and she brought a bit of sunshine back into my life. And then when Michael came back and then the *kinskinner* came along, well, my joy is pretty much complete. I couldn't ask for a better life."

Jaden nodded. *What would it be like to be normal?* To have a normal life like those around him? But a normal life would never, could never, exist for him.

"What about you? You got anyone?"

He shook his head. "*Nee.* Not really."

Paul happened to step outside just as Jaden was answering. "Don't let him fool you, Sammy. He's got his eye on my *schweschder*, Martha."

Sammy's brow rose. "Is that so?"

Jaden glanced at Paul, then at Sammy. "I'd rather not talk about it."

"I see." Sammy nodded.

"*Ach*, our ride's here." Paul turned and opened the door to Sammy's house. "Let's go, Silas. The driver's here."

Silas joined Paul outside. Both brothers bid them farewell before hopping into the car.

Sammy trained his gaze on Jaden again. "Let me know when you're ready to talk, *sohn*."

There was something about Sammy. He wasn't sure if kindred spirit was the right phrase, but it was pretty close. He felt like he could just sit and talk with Sammy for hours and share his whole life story with him.

He felt *safe*. And that was something he couldn't say he'd *ever* truly felt before outside the four walls of his home.

Could this man be an angel in disguise? *Ach*, Jaden wouldn't be surprised in the least.

TEN

"So, tell me your plans for this week." Josiah glanced at Jaden before shoving a pitchforkful of hay into one of the stalls.

"I don't have any plans." Jaden carried the bucket of fresh water to one of the stalls.

"What?" Josiah set the pitchfork down and wiped his sweaty forehead with his shirtsleeve. "I thought you were helping out at the school in Bontrager's district."

Jaden's lips pressed together. "Not anymore."

"Why?" His brother stared at him. "What happened?"

"I don't want to talk about it."

"No." His *bruder* frowned. "Jaden, you're not going to do this."

"Do what?"

"Shut everybody out like you always do."

"Like I *always* do? How would *you* know? You weren't even around for most of my life." He tamped down his ire.

"I was there for some of it. I've seen it enough to know."

"*Jah*, well. Some things are just better left unspoken."

"And some things need to be talked about. Talked through." Josiah insisted. "Didn't you go to the Millers' yesterday?"

"I did."

"And?"

"I had dinner with the family, and then I visited the schoolhouse with Martha." He shrugged.

"I don't understand. Why aren't you helping out there, then?"

"I blew it, okay?" He threw the bucket on the ground. "Are you happy now?" So much for restraining his anger.

"Easy, *bruder*." Josiah stepped near and squeezed his shoulder. "Tell me what happened. Please."

"I...I kissed Martha." He sighed.

"And?" His brother smirked, but he ignored it.

"Never mind. I guess you wouldn't understand."

"I'm trying to, if you'd just let me into your world."

He bent down and picked up the bucket he'd

thrown. "You don't want to be in my world."

"Fine. I'll let it go. But if you ever *want* to talk, I'm right here, Jade." Josiah touched his forearm. "Okay?"

"*Jah.*"

That morning, when Jaden had left the men's fellowship meeting at the Eichers', Sammy had encouraged him to read his Bible every day. He'd suggested starting in the book of Romans, saying it was full of hope and encouragement. And right about now, Jaden could use some of that.

Ach, he could hardly live with himself right now. What was wrong with him?

He opened the Bible Sammy had given him, although he wasn't sure where the book of Romans was. Studying the Scriptures for oneself had never been encouraged in his Amish *g'may*. He'd been admonished that those who studied too much would be filled with *hochmut*, pride. But Sammy seemed to know an awful lot about the words of *Der Herr*, and he hadn't seemed prideful about it at all. Jaden couldn't wrap his mind around a body *wanting* to study the Scriptures when they weren't in a position of leadership in the church. The thought befuddled him.

On the other hand, he could see that it had benefitted the men at the Bible study. None of them seemed to struggle like Jaden did. Not that their lives were perfect—they just seemed to know what to do when things got messed up. And he wanted to learn that too.

For the next half hour, Jaden shut himself in his room and read through the first chapter of Romans. But...where was the hope and encouragement Sammy had been talking about? He hadn't found any. *Nee*, what he'd found was condemnation and guilt. Eventually, he slammed the Bible shut.

Could it be that Sammy had suggested the wrong book? But, *nee*, he'd said Romans. Maybe Jaden had heard him wrong or had gotten confused when they'd been reading. Something wasn't clicking for him.

He huffed. He supposed there was only one way to find out, and that was to talk to Sammy again.

Hopefully, Josiah wouldn't mind if he left for a while. He needed answers. Or more accurately, he needed the hope and encouragement Sammy had been referring to.

"I see you've returned," Sammy smiled, holding the screen door open for Jaden to enter.

"*Ach*, it's quiet in here. Where is everyone?"

"Michael took his family on a picnic. It's the perfect day for it, ain't not?"

"It is, for sure." Jaden frowned. "Why didn't you go along?"

Sammy shrugged. "I felt like I should stay home." He smiled and his eyes connected with Jaden's. "Now I know why."

"So you stayed home because you..." Jaden shook his head. "It doesn't make sense."

"I've learned that I don't always know why *Der Herr* prompts me to do things. But if I follow His leading, I sometimes get to see His hand at work." Sammy glanced at the Bible that Jaden was holding. "I'm assuming you've come to see me?"

"I surely did."

"Well, then. Let me *chust* pour a glass of sweet tea for each of us and we'll sit out on the porch. How does that sound?"

Jaden smiled. "Great."

A few moments later, cups in hand, Jaden and Sammy sipped tea on the porch swing.

"Now," Sammy said. "Tell me what's on your mind."

Jaden shook his head. "I don't think you want to know everything that's on my mind."

"Try me." Sammy challenged.

"Seriously?"

"They call me the secret keeper. You tell me something, it will never pass my lips without your permission. Unless I'm talking to *Der Herr*, of course. But He already knows everything anyhow."

"You know how you suggested I read Romans?"

Sammy nodded.

"Well, I started today. And for the life of me, I can't find the hope and encouragement you mentioned." He shrugged. "I don't know if I'm reading it wrong or misunderstanding or...I don't know. But I've only read one chapter so far, so maybe that's why."

"What did you learn from the chapter you read, assuming it was chapter one?"

"It was." Jaden shook his head. "It was hard. I felt like it was condemning."

"Which part?"

Jaden opened the Bible to the place where he'd stuck a bookmark. He began reading silently, but couldn't get himself to utter the words aloud. He pointed out the passage he was referring to. "There. Verse twenty-seven. And then verse thirty-two."

Jaden braced himself while Sammy read the verses he'd indicated. *"And likewise also the men, leaving the natural use of the woman, burned in their lust one toward another; men with men working that which is unseemly, and receiving in themselves that recompence of their error which was meet."*

When Sammy finished, he looked at Jaden. But instead of seeing what he thought would be disapproval, he saw compassion. "*Sohn*, are you struggling with *this*?"

Tears pricked Jaden's eyes. He'd never spoken to anyone Amish about this. He'd never admitted it to anyone for fear of rejection. Anyone. And if anybody ever knew...

"I just, I don't know what to think about it." Jaden nodded and swiped away a tear, exposing his vulnerability. "I'm different. I think I might be gay, Sammy."

"And why do you think that?"

"Because that's how I feel. Like what you read in verse twenty-seven. That is what I'm attracted to."

"Did something happen to you, Jaden?" Concern reflected in Sammy's eyes.

"You mean, with another person?"

Sammy nodded. "A man?"

"*Jah*, but there were two of them. *Englischers*. Not men, but teenagers. I was younger yet. I didn't want to. I didn't feel like I had a choice. Or maybe I did, but I was just too scared to say no." He swallowed down his emotion. "So I pretended that I liked it, and it kept happening."

"*Ach, sohn.* I'm sorry." Sammy hung his head. "That should not have happened."

"This is how I am now, and I kind of feel powerless against it. But I know deep inside that it isn't right. Not just because of what verse thirty-two said and the verses I've heard about in the old testament. It's just something I've always known in my heart. I know it is wrong, although I have read things that say it is right and okay and a normal thing. But I am not convinced that it is."

Sammy set his tea down. "First of all, sin *is* a normal thing. We are *all* sinners. My sin might be different than yours, but the result is the same. We are both going against *Der Herr's* commands. We all struggle with one thing or another. The struggle itself is not a sin, but giving into it and allowing it to dwell in our hearts and minds is."

Jaden nodded.

"Paul Miller mentioned you were interested in a *maedel.* Is that true?"

"*Ach*, it is. And that's part of what makes it so confusing." He shook his head.

"Confusion comes from the evil one. The world tells us these things are okay, acceptable, and even to be celebrated. They say they are celebrating "love," but it is not love. *Gott* is love. And celebrating a sin that *Gott* tells us to abstain from—that He outright says is an abomination—is not love in any way, shape, or form. But that does not mean that *Gott* does not love them. He loved them—all of us—enough to shed His own blood. While we were yet sinners, Christ died for us. *That* is what love is, what love looks like.

"Satan is the god of this world and every chance he gets, he lies and deceives. His goal is to kill, steal, and destroy. He's brought many a *gut* man down. It started in the Garden of Eden. He lied to Eve and told her that the fruit was *gut*. He convinced her that something *Gott* had said was evil, was good. The devil wants to trip you up. He wants you to live in misery, a life of defeat. But *Der Herr* wants you to live the life He prepared for you. He wants you to live in victory."

"I don't know what that is or how to do it, Sammy."

"It is *Der Herr* that does it for you." Sammy held out his hand. "Let me see that Bible."

Jaden handed it to Sammy.

"Before I read these verses, I want to ask you something."

"Okay." Jaden blew out a breath, bracing himself.

"How do we know right from wrong, or good

from evil? Is it something we decide for ourselves or do you think it comes from somewhere or Someone else?"

"You had to go and ask an easy question." Jaden jested. "I think maybe it depends on what it is."

"What do you mean?"

"Well, I'm not sure there is a right and wrong to everything. Take my blue shirt, for example. Would it have been wrong for me to wear green today?"

Sammy chuckled. "You're right. No, we do have a lot of choices that don't directly involve right or wrong. But more specifically, I'm referring to morality. Like, say, stealing. Is stealing wrong?"

"*Jah.*"

"Why is it wrong?"

"Because you're taking something that doesn't belong to you. You didn't work for it, or earn it, and it wasn't given to you, so it's wrong. Not to mention, it's against the law."

"But what if a body was raised being taught it was okay?"

"It's still wrong."

"Why?"

"Because it's one of the Ten Commandments."

"But what if someone didn't believe in *Gott*? Is it okay for them?"

"No. It's never okay. And I don't think people have to believe in *Gott* to know that. It's just common sense."

"So would you say it's a natural law, a universal law?"

"*Jah*, I would. It's something that all humans know instinctively."

"Even little ones?" Sammy challenged.

"Maybe not at first, but they will learn without anyone telling them. Have you ever watched *bopplin* while they are playing? One will have a toy, then another one will come and take it. Then the one who had it in the first place will cry or hit or bite the one who took it. They know they've been done wrong."

Sammy chuckled. "That's a pretty *gut* illustration."

"I think I get what you're saying. We are not the ones who decide what is right and wrong, it is already decided for us."

"Pretty much. But also that truth itself is immutable. It isn't something that changes or can be changed. It is a constant. No matter what one's thoughts or feelings are on the matter. Does that make sense?"

"Yes. Definitely."

"Okay." Sammy held up the Bible. "Now that we've got that settled, I will show you what *Gott* desires for each of us."

Jaden watched as Sammy turned to a passage near the back of the book. How did he know where to find things so easily?

"I'm in 2 Peter 3. The context is the end of the world and *Der Herr's* coming, but *Gott* tells us His will in the second part of the verse. I'll *chust* read the whole thing. *The Lord is not slack concerning his promise, as some men count slackness; but is longsuffering to us-ward, not willing that any should perish, but that all should come to repentance.* So, you see, His will is that nobody perish and that everyone repent—"

"Perish? Does that mean to cease to exist?"

"In some cases, *jah.* In other cases, such as this one, it means to be lost eternally or to be sentenced to endless misery, according to Noah Webster."

"Yikes. That sounds disturbing. Scary."

"*Jah.* It is. Hell is for the devil and his angels. Which is why *Gott* made a way for anyone and everyone to escape it. We know this because of the verse I just read and because of what John wrote in chapter three of his Gospel. That is why Jesus Christ came, so that *all* people could be saved, if they choose to be. And it doesn't matter *what* they've done. We are *all* sinners, our sins are *chust* different."

"Why would anyone choose not to be saved from that?"

"Have *you* chosen?"

Jaden frowned. "What do you mean? I'm Amish."

"That's not what I'm referring to. And being Amish doesn't get you to Heaven any more than being in the barn makes you a horse." Sammy shook his head. "Let's go back to the book of Romans. Do you remember what you read?"

"Certainly not all of it."

"Paul said in verse sixteen, '*I am not ashamed of the gospel of Christ: for it is the power of God unto salvation to every one that believeth,*' and I'll *chust* stop reading right there. You see that? There's some of the hope and encouragement I was talking about. The Gospel of Christ, which Paul explains in 1 Corinthians 15, is this, '*That Christ died for our sins according to the scriptures; And that he was buried, and that he rose again the third day according to the scriptures.*' And Paul said that he wasn't ashamed because it meant salvation for everyone who believes it."

Jaden blew out a breath, trying to take in everything Sammy had just said.

"The hope and encouragement are that we don't *have* to die in our sins. We can secure salvation and escape Hell. Not only that, but we are free from sin. It no longer has a hold on us, if we are saved and belong to Him."

"But I don't understand how that can be."

"When you believe on the Lord Jesus Christ and are saved, something *wunderbaar* happens. The Holy Spirit, *Gott's* Spirit, comes and lives inside you. He gives you the strength you need to overcome temptation and sin. And guess what? The Bible says that if we resist the devil, he will flee from us." Sammy's smile stretched across his face. "Isn't that a *wunderbaar* verse?"

"So, if I believe in Jesus, I won't sin anymore?" His brow furrowed. That didn't seem right.

Sammy chuckled wryly. "*Ach*, if only it were that easy, *sohn*. I'm afraid not. While it is true that *Der Herr's* Spirit comes to live inside us, it is up to us to make the right decisions. It is still our choice. He is our guide. He shows us which way to go, but He does not force us to walk down the path. He will lead, but it's our choice to follow or no. Do you understand?"

"*Jah*, I think so."

"Someday, though, believers will get new bodies. And those bodies won't be subject to sin. *Ach*, won't that be a *wunderbaar* day?" Sammy sighed. "We must never put our confidence in the flesh, because the flesh will fail us every time. We must walk in the Spirit, and we must purpose in our heart to follow *Der Herr* and do what we know is right. The Apostle

Paul had the same struggle. You'll read about that in Romans seven."

"Romans again, huh?"

"Chock-full of *gut* stuff, it is."

"Sammy, how do I believe in Jesus? I mean, I *do* believe in Him. But I don't know if I'm saved. You know what I mean?"

"*Jah*, I think I do. That's how I was for years. I almost missed Heaven by twelve inches."

"What do you mean?"

"I believed with my head, but not with my heart. I had an intellectual knowledge of what Jesus had done." Sammy tapped his temple. "But not a personal relationship with Him. I never *received* Him." He placed his hand on his heart. "And that makes all the difference. The Bible says that even the devils believe and tremble."

Jaden nodded. "It makes sense."

"Now, listen to what the Bible says in—you guessed it, Romans again—it's in chapter ten this time." He opened the Bible. "*That if thou shalt confess with thy mouth the Lord Jesus, and shalt believe in thine heart that God hath raised him from the dead, thou shalt be saved. For with the heart man believeth unto righteousness; and with the mouth confession is made unto salvation.* Verse thirteen says, *For whosoever shall call upon the name of the Lord shall be saved.*" He looked at Jaden. "Just talk to *Gott*. Tell Him what's on your heart."

"Okay. Should I do it right here? Right now? In front of you?"

"Unless you'd rather have privacy. In that case, I could take a walk or go into the house."

"I don't mind you being here. Besides, you can help me if I say something wrong."

"*Ach*, it's not about speaking the right words. *Der Herr* is interested in what's in your heart. If you speak from your heart, that is all that matters."

Jaden blew out a breath, then bowed his head. "Dear *Gott*." And suddenly he was overcome with emotion. He couldn't utter another word. Instead, he wept for several minutes.

Sammy must've sensed Jaden's need for comfort because he pulled him close and held him until he'd silently told *Gott* everything on his heart.

When he nodded, Sammy released him.

"*Denki*." Jaden dried the last of his tears. *Ach*, he'd never cried so much in his life.

"You are now a child of *Gott*." Sammy smiled. "Welcome to the family."

"May I ask you something, Sammy?"

"Of course."

"Do you think I can ever have a normal relationship with a woman? As a husband?"

"With *Der Herr's* help, I believe you can. Remember how we talked about *Gott's* Spirit coming to live inside you? The Apostle Paul said, '*I can do all things through Christ which strengtheneth me.*' You can be sure that *Gott* is going to help you—from the inside out. Paul also said, '*I die daily.*' So I think what we need to do is ask *Gott* for His help and guidance every day, before our feet even hit the ground. Remember, *greater is He that is in you, than he that is in the world. Der Herr* is ready and waiting to help you."

Jaden released a sigh, then excitement began bubbling inside him. If Sammy thought he could build a real relationship with Martha, then Jaden believed it was possible too.

"*With Gott, all things are possible.*" Sammy patted him on the back.

ELEVEN

*J*aden felt like a new man as he traveled back toward his brother's house. Sammy had written down some Scripture references that he said would be helpful. One of them had really stuck in Jaden's head. Sammy said that he needed to remind himself of that verse every time his thoughts strayed.

He'd already begun committing the verse to memory, but he didn't know the whole thing by heart yet. He looked down at the verse. *"Casting down imaginations, and every high thing that exalteth itself against the knowledge of God, and bringing into captivity every thought to the obedience of Christ."* Now, if he could only remember that verse when the bad thoughts popped into his head.

Sammy's words echoed in his mind. "Remember, it is *Der Herr* who made them male and female at the beginning. He put them together in the garden, and designed each of them to complement each other perfectly. He is the one who created the family, and the *only* one who has the authority to define what the family is."

Jaden thought about Martha now. *Ach*, he needed to talk to her. He needed to make things right and restore their friendship.

"*Gott*, please help me. I don't want to fall again. Will You hold me up and guide me?"

Instead of going inside, he made his way out to the phone shanty. He'd call the Millers and see if Martha would talk to him. He picked up the phone and dialed the number, which was conveniently posted in the Amish directory his *bruder* kept in the small shanty.

"Hi, this is Jaden. Martha, will you please call me back today, if possible? I'll check the phone at noon, then again at two. Thanks." He gave the number, then hung up.

As he moseyed back toward the house, he thought on what he would say to Martha. He wasn't ready to—*ach*, the phone! He ran back toward the shanty. His *bruder* had said the answering machine was set to answer after five rings. He picked it up on the last ring, then tried to figure out how to turn the answering machine off.

The caller had hung up. He quickly dialed Martha's number again.

"Hello?" It was Martha!

"Martha, oh good, I'd hoped to reach you."

"Jaden?"

"*Jah*, it's me. Uh, listen. Are you available tomorrow afternoon?"

"Well, we don't have church this week, but my folks were planning to go visit with Silas's and Paul's families."

"Do you know what time you plan to return home?"

"Likely for supper, but I could take the pony cart separately then come home early. I mean, if you were thinking of coming by."

"Is two o'clock a *gut* time, then?"

"*Jah*, that should work fine."

Jaden couldn't stop from smiling. "*Gut*. I'll see you tomorrow at two, then. *Gott* willing."

"Okay."

"Goodbye." He waited until she responded, then listened for her end to click off.

Tomorrow afternoon couldn't come soon enough!

Martha hung up the phone, still stunned that Jaden had called.

Ach, had it only been yesterday when Jaden had kissed her? How many times had she relived that moment since then? More importantly, would he kiss her again? She couldn't stand to think about it. If she did, her heart would get all fluttery and her face would feel like she'd been cooped up in the schoolhouse in summertime with the doors closed.

Jaden was coming over! Tomorrow.

She needed to start thinking about something to make, because there'd be no cooking or baking on *Der Herr's* day. *Ach*, she could cook some of the corn Jaden had brought from his folks' place. And maybe she'd make some lemon poppyseed muffins. Jaden had mentioned liking lemon in one of his letters. She'd be sure to have some cold sweet peppermint tea ready too.

Martha hurried back to the house. She had a lot to do if she planned to help *Mamm* with supper and prepare everything for tomorrow. Her family would be surprised that she planned to take the pony cart to her *bruder's* house, but she didn't intend on telling them why she was coming back early. Unless it was absolutely necessary, like if one of her siblings insisted on riding back with her. *Nee*, that wouldn't do at all. She and Jaden would only have a few hours together as it was.

For sure, her family would think she and Jaden were courting if they returned home and found him there. Were they courting? She would do well not to assume anything. If Jaden only wanted to be friends, she'd have to be content with that. She really liked Jaden as a person, and although she desired to be more than friends, she'd take what she could get. She just hoped that if he ever *did* decide he wanted to court someone, that she would be his first choice.

Jaden pitched the last log of the stack at his feet into the horse-drawn wagon, while he waited for Josiah to finish up with the chain saw.

"I think this is all we're going to get to today. We've got supper, then you have your meeting tonight. You'll need to get washed up before then."

Jaden wiped the sweat from his brow. "*Jah*, you're right."

He walked over to where Josiah had just cut up a dead tree, then began loading the wood with his *bruder*.

"You seem different. Happier." Josiah lifted a half-smile.

"*Ach*, that's because I am." Jaden grinned.

"What happened?"

"Earlier, I went and talked to Sammy."

"So that's where you went." Josiah nodded.

"We had a *gut* talk. He's a very wise man."

"That, he is."

"He told me how to become a believer."

Josiah's brow arched upward. "And?"

Jaden couldn't hide his smile. "And I did."

"Really?"

"*Jah*, really." Warmth filled his heart. *Ach*, it was a *wunderbaar* feeling knowing he was saved and had a Helper in his corner.

"That's *wunderbaar, bruder*. I'm very glad to hear it. And I'm glad that you were able to work through whatever was bothering you."

"I plan to go see Martha tomorrow after church."

Josiah chucked the last log into the trailer. "Wow, you *did* work through whatever was bothering you. You were a mess earlier."

"Well, I'm still a mess. Kind of. I just know how to deal with it better now."

"I hear you. We all have our own struggles."

"Ain't that the truth?" He hopped on the back of the wagon just as Josiah coaxed the horses forward.

TWELVE

"This is my *bruder*, Jaden." Josiah introduced him to the community's leaders and schoolboard members. "Jaden, this is..." Josiah rattled off their names.

Jaden was grateful they'd agreed to a single meeting instead of two separate ones. "*Gut* to meet you. I'll try my best to remember your names." Maybe he should've written them down.

The men chuckled at his comment.

"You may have a seat." The minister gestured to the bench next to the dining table. "Josiah tells us you are single."

"I am." Jaden did his best to mask his nervousness.

"Any plans to settle down?"

"Well, seeing as I don't have a girlfriend or anything, no." He chuckled. "But I'm not ruling it out entirely. If *Der Herr* wants me to settle down, I'm sure He'll let me know."

The men laughed.

Ach, gut. They seemed to like him. Although, he was nervous as ever. He was thankful his *bruder* had come along.

"You taught school before?" The bishop asked.

"Yes. Well, briefly. It wasn't an entire school year, but I substituted for a few months while our teacher was recovering from an accident."

"And you had a *gut* experience?"

"I did. I think all the *kinner* liked me. The teacher had a schedule laid out, so I pretty much just went by that and picked up where she left off."

The men nodded.

"The children around here enjoy playing basketball and softball at recess. Do you play?"

"*Jah.* I enjoy basketball and softball too." He glanced at Josiah, who gave him a thumbs-up that only the two of them were privy to.

"Did you have any challenges or difficulties at the other school?"

"Nothing out of the ordinary, really. One time, we had an *Englischer* stop by and ask to see the school."

"And what did you say?"

"I informed them that we were in the middle of class and if they'd like to return after the scholars left,

I would be happy to show them the classroom. I also requested that they take no pictures of me or the children."

They glanced at each other, then at him, nodding satisfactorily.

One of the men slid a small stack of papers toward him. "Those are for you. It is information about the school, how many scholars we expect next school year, your pay schedule, the school calendar, the names, addresses, and phone numbers of the *kinner* and their families, should you need them, information on ordering books you might need. There's a catalog in there for the publishers as well."

"Do you have any questions?"

He tapped the papers. "Not that I can think of at the moment."

"So, you will start at the school this week, then?"

Jaden frowned. "*This* week?" *Ach, nee.* He was going to spend the week with Martha in her classroom. "I was under the impression it was next week. I already made plans for this week because I thought I'd be teaching the following week."

The men looked at each other.

"*Jah*, I guess that would be okay. That will give you a week, at least, to help out and get to know the scholars."

He thought about mentioning that he'd be helping Martha out at her school, but he wasn't sure that would go over very well with them. Especially since there'd been rumblings about distancing from Bontrager's district. If that ever happened...*ach*.

If that ever happened, he'd be stuck between a rock and a hard place. If this church district required complete abstinence between them and Bontrager's church, that would mean he would have to disfellowship with Martha and her entire family. That meant he and his *bruder* would no longer be permitted to commune with Silas, Paul, and Timothy in their men's group, which he wondered if the leaders were even privy to. He guessed not.

He needed to ask Josiah about it later. If he remembered, he'd bring it up at their next men's fellowship. Because this was something that really needed to be discussed, and prayed over. He couldn't imagine distancing himself from his friends, especially over something he wasn't sure he even believed in. Maybe he would talk to Sammy about that. The older man seemed to have answers to many of life's problems, or he knew where to find the answers. He was blessed to know Sammy, he realized. Not everyone had a go-to person who had all the answers, or seemed to, at least.

Jaden realized something just then. He was happy. For the first time in his life, he could say he was truly happy. The circumstances and possibility of turmoil around him didn't matter. Something inside him— was it *Gott's* Spirit that Sammy had talked about?— told him that no matter what happened, it would be okay. This must be what the word "peace" meant.

Really, it made no sense to human thinking. He *should* be anxious. He should be stressed. He should be fearful. But he wasn't. *Nee, Gott* had taken those things from his heart and replaced them with a tranquility he could not describe if he tried. It must be the peace that passeth all understanding.

He thought of some of the stories he'd read in the book *Martyr's Mirror.* Many of those slain for the cause of Christ had that peace in their hearts. No matter that the storm was raging around them, they'd kept their eyes on the Master of the sea. *Ach*, he must remember to never take his eyes off the Master. As long as he kept his eyes on *Him*, all would be well.

Der Herr was *gut* indeed.

"Well, that went well. I think." Josiah smiled as he guided the horse onto the road.

"*Jah*, I thought so." He stared out at the scenery as

they slowly passed by. Wildflowers were sprouting up from the ground, promising hope of new life. New life, like *Der Herr* had given him. Spring had to be the best time of year, to his thinking.

"You're awfully quiet over there. What are you thinking about, *bruder*?"

"*Ach*." He shrugged. "The goodness of *Gott*."

"*Jah*. We have a lot to be thankful for. Look at me. I'm back with the Amish again, something I *never* thought I'd return to. I have a beautiful wife and *kinner*. A grandchild on the way, even. A *wunderbaar* home. Great friends. I couldn't ask for anything more." Josiah shook his head. "I think of those people in other countries who have so little. I mean, for crying out loud, Bailey showed me some pictures where people were getting their water from a filthy river. Because of it, disease thrives. Can you imagine? Something as simple as water! We take it for granted every day."

"That's one of the things they're going on the mission for, right?"

"*Jah*. That, and they help build things, show them how to farm, and leave them with the Gospel. I don't think they really do much preaching or teaching, though. Our people tend to take a more silent, 'lead by example' approach. And leading by example is a good thing. But honestly, I don't know if it's enough. True, they *can* find Jesus by reading about Him from a pamphlet, but I know for myself, I really needed someone to explain things to me." He shrugged. "Not that everyone does."

"You're right. I understood things so much better when I sat down with Sammy and he showed me different Scriptures. But at least they're doing something, right? I'm sure those people will be grateful for the clean water and everything else."

"I just hate to see the missed opportunities, you know?"

"*Jah*, I get it. We will just have to pray that *Der Herr* will reach the people's hearts with what they *do* see and hear." Jaden nudged his *bruder* with his shoulder. "Sounds like you might want to go along, too."

"*Ach*, I couldn't leave Nora and the *kinner*. When you're married, a month is a *long* time to be away from your *fraa*."

"I can imagine." The corner of Jaden's mouth crept up as he thought of Martha.

"You thinking of settling down eventually?"

"Eventually, probably."

"I hear you have your eye on Silas's sister. I thought you said you were just friends."

"It's complicated."

"I see. Just kiss her again and voila, it won't be complicated anymore."

Jaden laughed. "That's what complicated things in the first place."

Josiah leaned to the side and eyed him. "Really? Did she slap you or something?"

"*Nee*! She kissed me back."

"Okay, then...I fail to see the complication. You like her, she likes you. Just roll with it. Move forward. What have you got to lose?"

"I don't want to lose her friendship. What if it doesn't work out? Or I do something stupid and mess it up?"

"If you do something stupid, then marry her. Problem solved."

"*Ach*, I wasn't talking about that."

"You befuddle me sometimes, *bruder*."

"How so?"

"Well, Silas's sister is...what? Thirty?"

"Thirty-one."

"Chances are she's looking to get hitched, sooner rather than later. You might run out of time."

"What do you mean?"

"If she's a *wunderbaar* woman, there's bound to be somebody interested in her."

Jaden shook his head. "There's no one else."

"Did she tell you that?"

"*Nee.*"

"Then how do you know?"

"I just do. I mean, she did kiss me back. She wouldn't have done that if there was someone else."

"True. But if you back off now, you may give someone else a chance to step in and steal her affections."

"Like who?"

"I don't know. I don't even know the woman. I'm just thinking in practical terms." Josiah eyed him. "Is she pretty?"

He smiled. "Very."

"I wouldn't take my time if I were you, *bruder*. You don't know what you got till it's gone. How would you feel if she announced her engagement in a few months?"

"I..." Jaden's mouth fell open, then shut. He shook his head. "*Nee.* That won't happen."

"Well, for your sake, I hope you're right."

THIRTEEN

*J*aden couldn't stop his fingers from tapping against his pant leg. *Ach*, were they only an hour and a half into the church service? *Jah*, it was halfway through, but the leaders mentioned something to him about introducing their new schoolteacher after the service. Which meant he would have to greet everyone. He had no idea how long he'd actually be here. All he knew was that he'd told Martha two o'clock and he couldn't—and wouldn't—be late.

Martha urged Sprinkles, their pony, to trot a little faster. She'd wanted to be plenty early so she'd have everything ready for when Jaden arrived. She was used to Quibble, her cantankerous former race horse, whom she often had to coax to slow down. It appeared that the two creatures were polar opposites.

Of course, she couldn't blame poor Sprinkles. Her legs were only so long.

The moment Sprinkles finally turned into the driveway, Martha groaned. A horse and buggy were waiting at the hitching post. *Ach*, had Jaden borrowed someone's rig and arrived early? On closer inspection, she noticed that it wasn't Jaden at all.

"*Hullo*, Martha." Titus Troyer stood next to his buggy, hat in hand. His clean blue shirt and black pants indicated this was likely a social call. He moved close as soon as she brought Sprinkles near to help unhitch the pony.

"*Ach*, Titus. Are you...what brings you by?" She slid out of the buggy and allowed him to care for Sprinkles.

"Well, I was talking to my cousin Amy." He eyed her carefully. "She said you *weren't* courting anybody, so I think maybe I misunderstood you the other day."

She knew she should have talked to Amy about Jaden. But when she shared things with her best friend, they had a curious way of slipping out into the community. And since she and Jaden weren't officially courting or anything, she didn't want to start any rumors. Especially ones that weren't true.

"Amy suggested I come by and have a chat with you." He glanced around. "Is it just the two of us here?"

"*Jah*, it is. But I'm expecting company in a little while." *Ach*, with Titus here, how would she find time to prepare for Jaden's visit? "I have a few things to do in the *haus*."

"I see." He nodded. "Well, don't let me stop you. We can talk inside."

Ach. "Uh, *jah*, okay."

She led the way into the house as soon as Titus put up Sprinkles and moved the pony cart to the carriage barn. The light seeped in from the windows, reminding Martha what a lovely day it was. She moved to the kitchen, then turned. "You may have a seat."

"*Denki.*" He pulled out the bench from under the dining table and made himself comfortable.

She didn't want to be rude by asking Titus to leave. Since he was a guest in her home and he'd come to see her, she needed to offer hospitality, as *Der Herr* required. "Where are the *kinner* today?"

"They're at *mei schweschder's haus* playing with *die kinner*."

She took out the pitcher of tea she'd prepared for herself and Jaden, and poured out a glass for Titus.

He smiled and took a drink. "*Denki.* It's *gut*."

She opened a bag of sweet and salty snack mix, poured some into a bowl, then set it near Titus.

He nodded his thanks, then pitched a small helping into his mouth.

"I hope you don't mind if I get some things ready for my guest." She hoped he'd get the hint.

"*Nee*, I don't mind." He didn't.

She blew out a breath. How long did he plan to stay for? She didn't want to be rude, but she also didn't want Jaden to show up when another man had come to call on her. *Ach*, it was a predicament indeed!

"So, about my offer—"

A knock on the screen door drew their attention. "Martha?"

Oh no. Jaden.

"I'll get it." Titus popped up from the seat before she had time to protest.

This was a nightmare. How was it that she hadn't had any suitors stop by for years on end and now there were two men coming to call on the same day? She supposed she should be pleased. Flattered even. Instead, embarrassment warmed her from the inside out. She rubbed her forehead.

FOURTEEN

"Hello, is Martha here?" Jaden eyed the bearded young man at the door. Who was he?

"*Jah*, she's just in the kitchen. We were enjoying a snack," he said.

We?

"Hi, Jaden." Martha offered a tentative smile as they neared the kitchen. Her cheeks were alive with color. *Ach*, she was so beautiful. "This is Titus. He just stopped by. His *dochder* is one of my scholars."

"And...your *fraa* is here too?" Jaden glanced around.

"*Ach, nee*. I'm afraid not. She passed on last year."

A widower? Here alone to see Martha? "I'm sorry to hear that," he managed to speak.

Josiah had been right. He wasn't the only one interested in Martha.

"I was just getting out the corn you brought from

your *mamm*." Martha smiled at him. "I thought you might want some."

He did. But he hadn't expected a threesome.

"Would you like some tea? I made peppermint." She gestured toward the table. "Feel free to have a seat."

"Sure. *Denki*." He took a seat across from Titus. *Ach*, this was awkward. "So, how old are your *kinner*?" Jaden didn't care for small talk, but he realized it was sometimes necessary. Like now.

"Two, four, and six. Two boys and a girl." He rubbed his beard, then glanced in Martha's direction. "Not easy raising them on my own."

"I can imagine." Jaden found himself feeling sorry for the guy, although he was an interloper. Or was *he* the interloper here?

"Well." Titus stood from the table. "I guess I should probably get going. I didn't realize Martha would have company today. I'll be sure to arrange things ahead of time next visit."

Next visit?

He waited for Martha to say something, but she remained silent. Why wasn't she telling this man how it was? *How was it, anyhow?* Jaden wasn't even sure himself.

She followed Titus to the door and thanked him for stopping by.

Jaden released a sigh of relief as soon as he heard the man's buggy leaving the driveway.

Martha turned, her look apologetic. "I didn't know he would be stopping by."

"Who is he?"

"Do you remember my friend Amy? You met her at the wedding. Titus is her cousin."

"I see." He eyed her carefully. "And he's obviously interested in you."

"*Jah*. He needs a *mamm* for his *kinner*." She admitted.

"I want to marry you," he blurted out.

Her gaze zeroed in on him. "What?"

"I mean...don't marry him. Marry me." He took her hand in his.

"I wasn't..." She shook her head. "Jaden. I don't...do you really mean that?"

"I don't mean right now, but eventually. Please don't marry him."

"Jaden, I never planned to marry Titus."

"You didn't? You don't?"

"*Nee*. And if I ever did consider marrying anyone, it would be you. But..." Her hand slipped out of his.

Worry furrowed his brow. "What?"

"I need to know. Why did you run away after kissing me the other day?"

Ach. He didn't want to share everything with Martha. At least, not yet. Not while their relationship was so fragile. Perhaps a half-truth would suffice? "I didn't want to ruin the friendship we had."

She frowned. "I don't think that's what it was. You can be honest with me, Jaden." Her gaze pierced his. How was it that she could see right through him?

"*Jah*, you're right. There's more to it. But I'm not ready to talk about it with you yet."

"Okay." She placed her hand on his upper arm. "Let me know when you are. I want to be there for you."

He nodded. "*Denki*." *Ach*, he loved this woman! "I did want to talk to you about something, though. Something important."

"Should we sit down?" She gestured toward the kitchen. "The corn can wait a few minutes, ain't not?"

"*Jah*." He followed her into the main room, then sat on the rocking chair opposite her. "I actually have a couple of things I'd like to talk about. First, I would like to help out in your classroom this week. That is, if you'll have me still."

"Of course. We would love to have you in the class." Her smile nearly stole his breath away.

"*Gut*." He glanced up. "Do you know Sammy Eicher?" Her browed creased.

"He's Mike Eicher's *grossdawdi*."

She nodded once. "I think I might have met him one time. He sounds familiar, but I'm not sure."

"Well, he's a very wise man, to my thinking. He knows a lot about *Der Herr* and *Gott's* Word. I guess you can say he's been mentoring me. Anyhow, he shared some Bible verses with me that really spoke to my heart. Do you...do you know what the Gospel is?"

"The Gospel? Do you mean the Bible?"

"*Nee*. I mean about Jesus Christ, and how He died for our sins and rose again."

"I know about it, *jah*."

"Well, I asked Jesus to save me. I've been born again. For real."

"That's what happens when you're baptized in the church, ain't not?"

"*Nee*." He shook his head. "This is different."

"I don't think I understand."

"I have a relationship with *Gott* now. He lives inside my heart."

Martha frowned. "I don't know what you mean by that. How can *Gott* live inside a person?"

"I'm not sure and certain how it all works, I just know that it does."

"How do you know? How can you know something like that?"

"Because He tells me what to do and what not to do. Like, if I'm about to do something that goes against His Word, I get a little nudge inside. He tells me that I shouldn't do it. And then if it's something right to do, He nudges me to do it."

Martha laughed.

"No, really. Like that guy, Titus." Jaden pointed toward the door. "I wanted to tell him to go take a hike and stay away from my girl. Instead, something inside told me I needed to be civil and kind. It wasn't easy."

She giggled.

"But when I read the Bible, the words seem to jump out at me. I'm trying to commit the verses to memory, because that's what we're supposed to do. That's one I already remembered. *Thy word have I hid in mine heart, that I might not sin against thee.*"

"That sounds amazing."

"It is, for sure. Do you want to meet Sammy?"

She shrugged. "*Jah*, sure. Or, you don't mean right now?"

"*Nee*. But someday."

"Okay." Her hands fidgeted. Was she nervous? "Are you ready for corn?"

"Sure. That sounds *gut*. But when we're done, I'd like to see that quilt you're working on."

Her cheeks darkened. "Uh, it's not done yet."

"That's okay. I didn't think it was."

She nodded slowly. "*Jah*, okay then."

She brought the corn to the table.

"Did you try some yet?"

"*Nee*, I was waiting to have some with you."

"What time is your family coming back?" He glanced toward the window.

"I imagine around four or five."

Jaden shot up from his seat and joined her near the stove. He stood behind her and slipped his arms around her waist. "*Gut*." He murmured in her ear.

She turned in his arms and stared up at him. "Why?"

He took two steps backward, pulling her with him, and lifted an eyebrow. "I think you know why."

She swallowed, then her gaze flicked to his lips.

It was all the invitation he needed. Instead of meeting her lips, his mouth went to her earlobe, then her neck.

"*Ach*, Jaden." Was she trembling?

He finally brought his lips down to slowly, gently taste hers. She grasped his vest, drawing him closer. He deepened the kiss, delighting that she returned his kisses with equal fervor. Exhilaration seemed to zing through every fiber of his being. Every second with

Martha was more *wunderbaar* than the one before. *Ach*, but he desired more. Much more. More than he should.

Casting down imaginations and bringing every thought in obedience...

Ach, why now? He complained.

He grumbled and forced himself away, although all he wanted to do was hold Martha in his arms. To indulge in the *verboten*. And if he'd read her actions correctly, he was quite certain she desired the same thing. *Which isn't gut*, he reprimanded himself. He shouldn't be causing Martha to sin.

Sorry, Gott.

"Let's..." He waited for his pulse to slow. "Have some corn now?" He hadn't meant for his voice to squeak.

Martha laughed. "*Jah*, I think corn is a *gut* idea."

FIFTEEN

Martha never dreamed she'd ever feel this way about a man. She was certain love was only for *other* people. But not her. Now that Jaden had stepped into her life, though, it seemed like loving Jaden—creating a life, a home with him—was all she *could* dream about.

He was the most handsome, most *wunderbaar* man she'd ever met.

"What was your life like back in Pennsylvania?"

"I think you already know from what I wrote in my letters."

"*Nee*. I don't mean that. I meant the time from when my family left Pennsylvania until we reconnected."

He shook his head. A frown etched on his face. "I don't think you want to know."

"Of course, I do. I want to know everything about you."

He seemed to study her. "Even the ugly parts?"

"If it's part of your story, part of who you are, then yes."

"*Jah*, okay. If you really want to know." He blew out a breath. "After what happened with Josiah, when we thought he died, and several families left, then my life kind of went downhill."

"*Ach*, I'm sorry."

"It wasn't your fault."

"What happened?"

"I just..." He stared off into the distance. "I met some people, I don't know if you could call them friends, but I thought so at the time. They were older than me and *Englisch*, so I thought they were cool. Anyway, they got me into things I wish I'd never known about. Then I eventually decided to distance myself from them, because I didn't like who I'd become, and sunk into a depression of sorts. Not many people knew about it. My folks may have had a vague idea, but it was mostly my own private pain."

Her hand covered his.

"I was seriously considering leaving the Amish life behind. I felt stuck, like my life wasn't going anywhere. You know what I mean?"

"*Jah*, I think so." She squeezed his hand. "What made you change your mind?"

"Josiah. Or maybe Bailey, I don't know. But for sure, it was *Gott* working."

"What do you mean?"

"Well, about that time when I was really thinking of leaving, a letter came for Josiah from Bailey. You know, he was *Englisch* at the time. But when I gave the letter to him, I told him that I'd been thinking of jumping the fence. He'd said something to me. He said that I should consider if that was what I really wanted to do. Because if I did leave, my life would never be the same again. And I asked if that was a *gut* thing or a bad thing. He told me it was both. And I began wondering if it was really worth it. Leaving my parents and family behind...

"For the most part, I'd already overcome my depression, but I was bored with life. So I decided to stick it out to see what might lie up ahead. I threw myself into work so I didn't have much time to think about my restlessness. I figured there must be *something* waiting for me in the future."

She pressed her lips together. "Did you ever have an *aldi*?"

"*Nee*, not really. I drove a couple of girls home, but I never felt a real interest in them. Not until I reconnected with you." He smiled, then kissed the top of her nose.

"And now...you're happy?"

"*Ach*, Martha. I never dreamed I could be this content. And, *jah*, part of it is being with you. But finding *Gott* has made everything that's happened in my life worth it. I know that life won't ever be perfect, and I'm not expecting it to be. But, I know that whatever happens, I have *Der Herr* to help me through it now. And that makes all the difference in the world."

She snuggled close to him, loving the feeling of his arms around her. "I'm glad."

"Me too." He leaned down and met her lips. "Will you show me your quilt now?"

"Yeah, sure." She stood from the couch and reached for his hand to pull him up. Instead, he pulled her back down onto his lap and kissed her ever so sweetly. *Ach*, she would give this man the world if he asked and it was in the power of her hands to do so.

"I couldn't resist." He grinned, a hint of mischief sparkling in his eyes. "*Kumm*, let's go see your quilt."

Martha led the way to the *dawdi haus* where she and *Mamm* had set up their quilting frames. When her *bruder* Paul moved out, they'd moved them in. The main room was the perfect place, really, since they didn't need to be moved and they weren't in the way. The lone bedroom remained furnished, but unused.

"This one is mine." She touched her quilt and

attempted a demure smile. She found it difficult to remain humble when it was turning out so *wunderbaar*.

"*Ach*, you're making it in my favorite pattern?" His eyes widened.

She ducked her head. "*Jah*."

"And my favorite colors?"

She nodded.

He studied her, shaking his head. "It's *wunderbaar*."

"Do you think so?"

"*Ach, jah*, it's perfect."

"*Gut*. Because I was making it for you."

"For *me*? Really? *This* is for *me*?"

"I wanted to do something for you." She shrugged. "I'd hoped to have it finished before you saw it."

"*Ach*, Martha. This is amazing." He fingered one of the blue and teal stars. "You're...well, I don't really have words for you right now. I mean, to describe how spectacular you are. I can't believe you're making this for me."

"I hope you like it."

"Like it? I'll cherish it. *Ach*, the hours you've been pouring into this thing." He enclosed her in his embrace, as though he never wanted to let her go. "I don't deserve you."

"I feel the same way about you."

"*Nee*. I *really* don't deserve you."

SIXTEEN

Commotion in the main house drew their attention. Jaden glanced toward the door as soon as he pulled his needle through the quilt, a secret smile playing on his lips.

"*Ach*, my family must be back." Martha's voice quivered.

He stood and rounded the corner of the quilt frame, then laid his hand over hers, attempting reassurance. "It's okay, *schatzi*," he whispered.

She swallowed and nodded. "We should probably go back into the *haus*. Besides, we maybe shouldn't have been working in here on the Lord's day, ain't not?"

"It wasn't all work. We were having fun, ain't not?" His brow rose a smidgen.

Her gaze collided with his, and they shared a grin.

He cleared his throat. "Besides, my *mamm* never

considered quilting on the Lord's day to be work, but if your folks are against it then we can quit."

"We should probably join them, I think." She stood from her quilt-side perch.

"*Jah*, okay. Where should I put my needle and thread? Should I just leave it there? Do you want me to snip it off?"

"*Nee*, you can just leave it there."

"Maybe we can work on it again after school tomorrow," he said, clearing his throat.

"Would you want to?" She stood and walked to the *dawdi haus* door that connected the two dwellings.

He followed her through the door into the main house. "Work on the quilt? Sure."

"*Ach*, I didn't know Jaden was here." Her *mamm's* eyes lit up.

"*Jah*." Nervousness accompanied Martha's response. "I was...uh...showing him my quilt."

Emily exchanged a suspicious look with her older sister, Susan. *Nee*, surely they couldn't perceive what they'd been up to. *Could they?* He swallowed.

Mamm nodded. "Bailey and Timothy are joining us for supper."

"Well, I warmed up plenty of corn. So we can have sandwiches with it," Martha suggested.

"I haven't seen either of them since I arrived." Jaden smiled.

"I know Bailey will be happy to see you," Emily said. "Did she know you were coming to visit Indiana?"

"Visit?" He shot a questioning glance at Martha.

"*Ach*, I haven't told them." Martha admitted.

"Told us what?" Emily thrust a hand onto her hip.

"Jaden's moving to his *bruder's* Amish district. He's going to be the school teacher there next year." Martha smiled.

Emily snorted. "You're pulling one over on us."

Martha's hands lifted. "I'm not. For real. Ask him yourself."

Jaden chuckled. "Every word your *schweschder* said is true."

Emily's jaw dropped. She looked back and forth between the two of them. "So...does this mean...?" A knowing smile lit her countenance.

"Wouldn't you like to know?" Martha winked at Jaden, then she turned to her folks. "Jaden and I are stepping out for a walk."

"Take your time. Your *schweschdern* can help put supper on the table. Just be back when Bailey and Timothy arrive."

"Okay." Martha waited by the door while Jaden fetched his hat.

As soon as they stepped out the door, Jaden laughed with Martha. "I guess we're giving them something to talk about, ain't not?"

"For sure. Goodness, nobody in this family minds their own business. Except *Dat*, maybe."

"I like your *dat*. He seems very easygoing."

"*Jah*. He's a lot like you. Or you're a lot like him, I should say."

He lifted his head, allowing the breeze to caress his face. "Where are we going?"

"I thought we'd walk down by the pond."

"That sounds *gut*. Any fish in there?"

"I think maybe a few, but *Dat* and the *buwe* would go down to the stream to fish."

"Does it freeze over in the winter?"

"Most years, *jah*. But it never lasts long enough." There had been a wistfulness to her words.

"Do you ice skate?"

"*Jah*, we play hockey. It's a lot of fun."

He glanced toward the house once they were out of sight, then he reached for her hand. "I'm excited about school tomorrow. What time do you need me to be there?"

"Eight should be fine. The scholars arrive between eight and eight thirty."

"I'll come at ten till eight, then."

"I can't wait." Martha smiled.

"The weather is so nice here. It isn't as humid as Pennsylvania."

"*Nee*, it isn't, but it does get humid when the temperatures rise. And you've got to look out for tornados here. Does your *bruder's* house have a basement?"

"You know, I'm not sure. I thought everybody out here had basements."

"Many do, but not everyone. I'm glad our house has one."

"Have you ever had to use it during a tornado?"

"Mostly not, but a couple of times we did when it got real stormy and the sky was making strange noises."

"*Ach*, I think I might too if I heard the sky talking to me." He chuckled.

"We usually just enjoy the storms, though. Sit outside on the porch and watch them. There's some pretty fantastic lightning. One time, it hit one of the trees. The thunder was so loud and it shook the whole house."

"Yikes."

"*Jah*, I'm glad it didn't strike our home."

"Me too."

"Kayla, Silas's *fraa*, said they hardly ever got any

storms in the area she was from in California. And never thunder and lightning like out here. I think the storms here might scare her sometimes."

"No thunder and lightning?"

"Well, yes some. But it just wasn't as boisterous or as frequent as it is here."

"I think I hear a buggy coming up the road. Do you think it might be Timothy and Bailey?"

"There's a *gut* chance. We should probably go back now."

"In a minute." He pulled her behind a tree. "You need a kiss first."

"I do, huh?" She grinned.

"*Jah.* You most definitely do."

SEVENTEEN

*J*aden and Martha stayed out a little longer than they anticipated, so Bailey and Timothy beat them to the house. They were sure to put proper distance between them before entering the Millers' home. Hopefully, the family hadn't begun supper without them.

"*Onkel* Jaden!" A smile burst out on Bailey's lips the moment she spotted him coming through the door.

"How's my oldest niece?"

"As much trouble as ever." Her husband Timothy teased. Jaden noticed his faint blond facial hair had begun filling in.

"He's right." Emily joined the conversation. "She's been a bear lately."

"I have not." Bailey protested, fastening her arms over her chest.

"You have too. Don't deny it." Emily set a loaf of bread on the table, along with some sliced meat. "*Kumm* sit. It's ready now."

Martha's family, along with Jaden, Timothy, and Bailey, all sat quietly around the table while Martha's father said the silent prayer. As soon as he cleared his throat, the food was passed around to each person.

"This corn is *gut*." Bailey's father commented.

Jaden smiled. "When do you all leave for the mission?"

Bailey groaned. "Let's not talk about the mission."

"It's still a *gut* thing, even if you're not going," Susan said. She glanced at Jaden. "We leave in about three weeks."

"*Ach*," Emily gasped. "Did you hear what Silas said about Josiah's church?"

Her father chuckled. "I don't think Josiah Beachy has a church." He winked at his youngest *dochder*.

"You know what I mean, *Dat*. Bishop Detweiler's church, whatever." Emily sighed. "They might be breaking fellowship with us because of the mission thing."

"*Ach*," Martha said. "Is that true, Jaden?"

Jaden shrugged. "I don't know much about it, but Josiah did mention it to me before I moved here. Said it might be a possibility but nothing had been set in stone yet."

"But if they break fellowship with us, then..." Martha let her voice trail off. She stared at Jaden, then he noticed tears filling her eyes.

Ach. He wished he could take her in his arms right now and hold her close. "*Der Herr* will work everything out." He attempted to assure her.

"They're not going to keep me from seeing my *dat* and siblings, that's all there is to it." Bailey insisted.

"I'm afraid we are not the ones to make the rules, child. We *chust* have to abide by them." Martha's father reminded her.

"Well, I'm sure *Dat* will just move to our district then," Bailey said.

Jaden grimaced. "Honestly, I don't know what will happen, Bailey. Nora's pretty ingrained in Detweiler's church. Her folks are there. Not to mention she and Miriam Eicher are best friends. Then there's Michael and Sammy, too."

"Let's *chust* pray about it. There's no need to worry." Martha's father advised. "Like Jaden said, *Der Herr* will work everything out."

It was true that Jaden had said the words, but that didn't mean the leaders in his *bruder's* district would make the right decisions. If they chose to disfellowship with Bontrager's community, they wouldn't be the first family broken up by the rules of the Amish church. Jaden just prayed that his and Martha's relationship would survive the tumultuous time that might possibly lie ahead for them.

"You've been quiet." Jaden spoke the words into Martha's prayer *kapp*.

"*Jah*." She leaned back, staring up at him. She couldn't help the tears that had gathered on her lashes. *Ach*, she couldn't lose Jaden. He was the best thing that had ever happened to her. "What is going to become of us, Jaden?"

He sighed. "Nothing *Der Herr* does not allow, I assure you. We can trust Him, Martha."

"It would be a hard thing, for sure. If they *do* require you to shun Bontrager's *g'may*, then you will have no choice."

"Martha, there is always a choice. Let me just say right here, right now, I choose us."

"But then you wouldn't be allowed to fellowship with your *bruder*. And you'd lose your job. I wouldn't want that for you."

"Jobs are everywhere. And my *bruder* will do what he feels is right for himself and his family. I will respect whatever decision he makes, *if* it ever comes to that. Let's not borrow trouble. Let's be thankful for the blessings *Der Herr* has given us today and let Him worry about tomorrow."

"I don't think *Der Herr* worries."

"Exactly. And neither should we. He is in control." He caressed her cheek with his thumb. "Well, a week helping out here, then a week helping at the school in my *bruder's g'may*, and we'll be finished for the summer."

"*Jah*. I'm excited for Susan and Nathaniel. It will be a *wunderbaar* experience to get to see another part of the world, I'm thinking."

"For sure. It will be *gut* for them to see how other folks live."

"Do you think it's as bad as they say?"

"It's likely worse. I'm surprised your *schweschder* Emily isn't going along too."

"*Nee*. She's tending to her garden and her roadside stand. She's pretty excited about it since she gets to keep whatever she makes. It's pretty much the highlight of the year for her." Martha laughed.

"Would you ever consider going on a mission trip?"

"I think I might. What about you?"

"*Jah*, I think I would like to. But I guess it's too late to go on this one, since you need a passport and all."

Martha nodded. "It takes a while to get one. I think

Susan's and Nathaniel's took about five weeks. But you can pay extra money and it will arrive faster. I still don't know if it would arrive on time for the trip, though."

"Maybe next year, then, if they go again."

"We could plan on it." She smiled, thinking on the future. Their future. *Ach*, a future with Jaden at her side seemed like a dream. But, would her and Jaden's love survive the potential difficulties life could throw their way? With all her heart, she'd prayed it would.

EIGHTEEN

Jaden grinned as his driver pulled onto the side of the road near the schoolhouse. "Thank you. If you could pick me up around seven at the house you dropped me off at yesterday, that would be great."

"No problem. See you then," Mr. Sample said. "You looking for a ride here all week?"

"I think so."

"I'm your man. Just give me a call. But let me know as soon as possible because my schedule fills up pretty quickly. I'm wide open right now."

"Go ahead and jot me down then. If, for whatever reason, I need to cancel, I'll give you a call."

"Sounds good. Have a great day!"

"You too." He slid out and shut the car door.

He noticed smoke billowing from the chimney. *Ach*, he should have come earlier to start the fire for Martha. He hadn't realized she would need one, but he supposed it was a little nippy this morning.

As he approached the schoolyard, he saw that there were two buggies in the side yard. Had some of the scholars already arrived? It was quite early yet. They still had over a half hour until school began.

The door to the schoolroom opened just as he began walking up the steps. The widower, who'd been visiting Martha before he arrived yesterday, stepped out the door.

"Goodbye, Titus." Jaden heard Martha's voice echo from inside the schoolhouse. "*Denki* for starting the fire this morning."

Jaden nodded to the man as they passed each other on the steps.

"You visiting Martha today?" Titus stopped and turned. His eyebrow quirked.

"I'm helping her teach the scholars this week."

"*Ach*, I hadn't known. Are we getting a new teacher yet?"

"*Nee*, I'll be teaching in Detweiler's district."

"I see."

Jaden wanted to get this conversation over with. "Have a *gut* day." He tipped his head, dismissing the man.

"I'll be stopping by to drop off *mei dochder* in a while yet, so I'll be seeing you again." Titus trudged down the steps toward his buggy.

Should he set things straight with the man, so he'd quit pursuing Martha? It seemed like he might have to.

He yanked the door open. He shouldn't be frustrated, but he was anyhow. Thinking of another man pursuing Martha set him on edge. *You're jealous. Jah*, he supposed he was. He growled before stepping into the classroom.

"*Ach*, you just missed Titus Troyer," Martha said.

"I passed him on his way out." He frowned. "I could have started the fire for you. I can come earlier tomorrow. I hadn't known you'd need one."

"Titus was already here when I showed up and he offered to do it. I didn't want to hurt his feelings since he came all this way."

"Alone." Jaden frowned.

Her cheeks darkened. "*Jah*."

"Are you going to inform him that we're seeing each other, or do you want me to? Because I don't like him hanging around you all the time."

"*Ach*, it's not a bother, really. I feel bad for him. He's lonely." She turned and began writing on the chalkboard.

Heat spiraled through his veins. "You said he was looking for a *fraa*."

145

"He is."

He didn't like talking to her back. Was she avoiding him? "Martha."

"He's a nice man. You don't have to worry about him making a pass at me."

"Making a pass at you?" His voice screeched. "I'd knock him into next Tuesday, if he did."

Martha gasped, then turned around. "What is this, Jaden? What's wrong?"

"What's—Martha, I thought *we* were courting, ain't not?" He removed his hat and slid his hands through his hair.

"*Jah*, we are."

"Well, then? What? You just enjoy his attention? Or do you enjoy seeing me get upset?" He resisted the urge to throw his hat down.

"Fine, I'll tell him." She turned back around and began writing on the chalkboard again.

"No. I need to know what's going on here." He moved close and touched her shoulder. "Is he courting you too?"

"*Nee*. I told you it was nothing. I just don't want to hurt his feelings. He already lost his *fraa*. I just feel bad for him. And if coming over here to start a fire for the *kinner* makes him happy, then I don't want to douse that little bit of happiness."

"I get it. I do. But don't you see, Martha? He's not coming over here for the *kinner*, he's coming for *you*. And it's not fair to him—or me—to allow him to continue this. You're giving him false hope that he has a chance with you."

"I'll talk to him after school." She frowned, but he noticed that her eyes glistened.

Ach, this was not how he'd anticipated beginning his first day of teaching with Martha. "I'm sorry, Martha. I didn't mean to get upset."

She swiped under her eyes, then straightened. "The *kinner* are here now."

When Martha dismissed the *kinner* for recess, frustration with Jaden still gnawed at her. She had not been expecting this controlling, jealous side of him. And it bothered her.

Why couldn't he trust her? Didn't he know that he held her heart in the palm of his hand? That she didn't have the slightest bit of interest in Titus Troyer? Had Jaden actually believed she was courting Titus too? She thought she'd made that abundantly clear to Jaden when Titus had left the house the other day, but apparently, she hadn't been clear enough.

Could the *kinner* sense the friction in the air? If so,

it hadn't been reflected in their actions. In fact, they seemed to be on their best behavior.

She glanced out the window as Jaden shot a basketball into the hoop on their small basketball court, then passed it off to one of the *buwe*. He was really *gut* with the *kinner*. Detweiler's district would be blessed to have him teach their scholars. He connected effortlessly with the *kinner*. He seemed to be a natural.

NINETEEN

Martha held the reins as the passenger side of the buggy dipped and Jaden hopped in.

"You sure you don't want me to drive?" He offered.

"*Nee*, I got it. Quibble can be a pain sometimes." She gently pulled the reins, backing out of the schoolyard, then turned onto the road. The thing she liked about this country lane was that few cars traveled it. The thing she didn't like was that there were no painted lines, so Quibble tended to tread the middle.

The former racehorse trotted as they sat in silence. She supposed each of them were lost in their own thoughts. They still hadn't discussed what happened that morning. The *buwe* had been intent on their "new teacher" taking lunch with them, so she and Jaden really hadn't had any time alone after the *kinner* arrived. Till now.

The sound of a car approaching told her she needed to move Quibble to the side. She adjusted the reins, but the stubborn horse refused to veer right. "*Ach!*" She reached for the whip they kept on the buggy for such instances.

"*Nee.*" Jaden frowned and stopped her from grasping it. He gently took the reins from her and directed the horse to the right side, while the *Englisch* vehicle passed in the other lane.

Martha gasped. "Now, why wouldn't he do that for me?"

"He's upset with you right now, because you're upset. He can sense it and he's mimicking your behavior."

"No, he isn't. No, I'm not."

His sideways glance told her he didn't believe her words.

"Okay, maybe I am *a little* upset. Can you blame me?"

"Let's wait till we get to your place to have this conversation, okay?" He nodded toward the horse.

"Fine." She crossed her arms over her chest and stared out at the passing scenery. She didn't like this one bit.

"I think the scholars took to me well enough." He changed the subject. Smart man.

"They loved you. I knew they would. You're a natural in the classroom."

He flicked a glance at her. "Do you think so?"

"*Jah*, I do." She looked at the reins in his hands. "Does it feel weird being on the passenger's side and holding the reins?"

"It does." He smiled. "I'd suggest we switch spots, but if somebody happens by and sees you in my lap, they might get the wrong idea." He chuckled.

"*Ach*, Jaden!" She swatted his arm.

"Hey, you mentioned it."

"*Jah*, but my mind didn't go *there*. Well, until you brought it up." She shook her head.

"I'm afraid my mind goes there too much." He frowned. "How's that for honesty?"

"I suspected it did." She swallowed. "You tend to get carried away when we kiss."

"I know. I'm sorry. Just elbow me in the ribs next time."

"Ow! That would hurt."

"It would get me to stop, at least."

"Well, I didn't ask you to stop. I could have." Her cheeks warmed and she flicked a glance at him. "So, I guess it's my fault too."

"I don't ever want to make you uncomfortable, so if I'm being too aggressive, then tell me."

"Okay."

"*Ach*, the conversations teachers have." He teased.

"I hope I'm the only teacher you'll ever have *this* conversation with."

"Likewise." He winked, then opened his palm toward her.

She slid her fingers between his, loving the feel of her hand in his. "Are you staying for supper?"

He maneuvered the horse into the driveway. "If you'll have me."

"I'll always have you."

His thumb lightly caressed the top of her hand, before he put proper distance between them. "I hope so."

"Let's go for a walk." Jaden suggested, the moment they set their school supplies down inside the house.

"We have papers to grade, ain't?"

"*Jah*, but they can wait. We have more pressing matters to discuss." He attempted a sad smile, hoping they wouldn't argue. He hated arguing with Martha.

"Let me tell *Mamm*, in case she needs me."

He nodded. "I'll meet you outside."

Jaden waited on the porch a few minutes, but Martha seemed to be taking her sweet time.

Restlessness took him hostage. He moseyed on over to the barn, wondering if her father and *bruder* were home. She'd mentioned in one of her letters that they sometimes worked on construction projects.

He spotted her *bruder* working in the haymow, sleeves rolled up exposing his muscled forearms, moving bales of hay. Jaden stood staring for several moments, lost in thought. He tended to do that now and again. He didn't want to bother him, so he remained silent.

"Don't look at me like that." Nathaniel's irritated voice pulled him from his trance.

"Like what?"

"You *know.*" Nathaniel stood, staring down at him with his fists on his hips. "I've seen your kind before."

"No, I don't *know.*" But he did. He would never admit it to Nathaniel, though.

"Whatever." Nathaniel gestured toward him and shook his head. "Just don't. Don't you *ever.*"

Jaden felt like hollering, but he wouldn't. What would Martha think? *Ach.*

Casting down imaginations...You have to help me, Gott!

"You ready?" Martha's voice called from behind.

He spun around and hurried toward her. "*Jah,* let's walk."

153

He needed to get as far away from Martha's *bruder* as possible. If Nathaniel called him out in front of his sister, Jaden would flat out deny it. *Jah*, he'd be lying. But Martha couldn't know. She could never know.

"Let's go down by the pond?" he suggested.

"Okay."

They made their way beyond their wooded area until they came to the pond. "Let's sit on the grass."

She stared down at the grassy area and worried her lip. "I should have brought a blanket out."

"We could just stand, then. Or..." He lifted his eyes from Martha long enough to see their surroundings. "Hey, I didn't know there was a boat out here."

"*Dat* or Nathaniel must have brought it out."

He tapped the side of the boat, eyeing it cautiously. "Is it sturdy? Do you think it would hold us?"

"*Jah*. Probably."

"Let's sit in the boat then." He grinned. "Want to take a ride? I know how to row."

She shrugged. "Sure."

"Does your *dat* plan to build a dock?"

"I'm not sure." She stepped into the boat while he held it steady.

He gave the boat a little shove from the shore, then hopped in. He used the oars to push away from the bottom of the pond until they were far enough away to actually float on the water without touching the sediment underneath.

He lifted his face to soak in the rays of sunshine. "This is nice, ain't not?"

"It is." She released a breath. "Did you want to talk now?"

"*Jah*. I think you already know how I feel."

"I do."

"And?"

"I think you know how *I* feel."

"Okay, we can't do this. We're not getting anywhere." Jaden rubbed his forehead. "What do you want from me? Do you want me to just turn a blind eye when some other man is trying to steal my girl? I'm sorry, but that's not going to happen."

"He was just doing a kind deed."

"Stop defending him. That's not what he was doing. He's trying to win your affections."

"Jaden, I don't like this. I don't like that you feel that you can't trust me."

"I trust you." The words rushed out.

"Then step back and let me handle Titus. Okay?"

He forced his lips together. He didn't want to agree. But he also didn't want to make Martha upset with him. "Fine. You take care of it."

"In my own time."

Ach. He wanted to protest so badly. Instead, he nodded in silence.

"Another thing. I can't have you trying to control my every move. I'm a teacher. I'm going to talk to men once in a while. I can't have you getting jealous every time that happens." She covered his hand with hers. "Do you understand?"

He nodded again, not trusting himself to speak.

"I'm sure that once you start teaching, you will be talking to many women. And not just the *mamms*, older *schweschdern* too. I'd be a mess if I freaked out every time you talked to one. So let's just decide we're going to trust each other. Can we do that?"

"Okay, I'll do my best."

"That's all I ask."

"But..." He clamped his mouth shut. He wouldn't say another word about Titus. He'd just ignore the fact that he was pursuing Martha. But she was right. He needed to trust her to do the right thing. Just like *she* was trusting *him* to do the right thing. Even though she knew nothing about his real struggles.

"Should we row this boat back to the shore? I should probably help *Mamm* and *mei schweschdern* with supper. Maybe you can help *Dat* and Nathaniel outside. Or you could start correcting papers."

"I'll correct papers." Because he was quite certain Nathaniel didn't want to be around him. Hopefully, her *bruder* would keep his suspicions to himself.

TWENTY

The week helping out in Martha's classroom had flown by way too fast for Jaden's liking. He found himself wishing he could stay there full time, but he knew his obligations were elsewhere.

He'd soon begin his real internship with the teacher in Detweiler's district. And honestly, he wasn't really looking forward to it. Hopefully, his attitude would change on Monday. He guessed it was probably just nerves making him second guess himself. He *had* enjoyed teaching this week.

"I know the *kinner* are going to miss having you helping out in the classroom. Especially Silas's and Paul's *kinner*." Martha smiled. "Daniel asked if he could call you *Onkel* Jaden. I think he must've suspected we were courting."

"*Ach*, really?" Jaden's smile widened as he picked up the last of the reading books and placed them back on the shelves. "I like your family. A lot."

Except for Nathaniel. Up till now, her *bruder* hadn't said anything more, but Jaden didn't trust the man. And Nathaniel made no qualms about letting Jaden know his disdain for him. Jaden tried to avoid him like the plague.

"Two more weeks for the mission trip, ain't not?" He'd be glad to have her brother gone, so he'd have some breathing room. As it was, Jaden felt like Nathaniel watched him like a bird of prey staring down at him from a tree just waiting for his demise so he could swoop in and... Jaden shook his head. He really shouldn't be having uncharitable thoughts toward someone he barely knew.

"*Jah.* Susan's really excited. It's all she talks about." She swept between the desks.

His brow quirked. "And your *bruder*?" He held the dustpan to scoop up the debris she'd swept.

"Nathaniel, not so much. Seems like he's had something on his mind lately."

Jaden rubbed his forehead. He needed to have a chat with her *bruder* whether either of them liked it or not. For crying out loud, he'd looked at the guy a little too long. That was it. Sometimes he thought it might be better if he could just pluck his eyes out.

God, I can't do this on my own. I need You.

At least tomorrow was Saturday. They'd have their men's fellowship and he'd be able to talk with Sammy again. He supposed he could stop by any time he pleased, and maybe he should, given the circumstances. He needed someone in his court, and he felt like Sammy was that person. The one person who seemed to understand and didn't judge him for his shortcomings and failures.

"I'm going shopping tonight to look for a few things for the classroom. I'm sure *Mamm* will want me to get groceries too, while I'm there. Do you want to come with me?" Martha's words pulled him from his musings.

He finally dumped the contents of the dustpan into the trash can. He'd empty it on their way out.

"*Jah*. That sounds *gut*." Spending time with his girl *always* sounded *gut*.

"Why don't we go as soon as we get home, then we can be back for supper? Does that sound fine?"

"*Jah*. Or we can eat out. I wouldn't mind taking *mei schatzi* to a restaurant." He raised his eyebrows twice.

"That might be nice."

"Well, I don't know the area at all, so I would have no idea where to go."

"There's a Chinese buffet that's popular, if you're

really hungry. They have all kinds of food, not just Chinese."

He smiled. "A buffet? Sounds *gut* to me." Of course, there was rarely a time when food in general *didn't* appeal to him.

"Great. Let's go."

"So, what are we looking for again?" Jaden perused the children's books.

"Just something fun for the little ones. Maybe books about cats or dogs or horses. Nothing too fancy, though."

"Not like this?" He teased, showing her a book with an unrealistic looking animal with eyes half the size of its large head and a tiny body.

She shook her head. "Strange, ain't not?"

He chuckled. "Someone must buy them or they wouldn't be here, I reckon."

Jaden turned the corner into the next aisle of the small book section. Unwittingly, he allowed a bodybuilding magazine to catch his eye. He looked away, attempting to denounce the attraction he felt to the handsome man featured on the front. Next to it, there was a magazine with a man waving a rainbow flag. He'd known all about the symbol, thanks to his "friends." He never understood how a rainbow could stand for something *Der Herr* was against, when He was the one who created it in the first place.

Nee, Gott had said it was a sign of His promise to never flood the entire earth again. But it wasn't only a symbol of that, it was a grave warning against sin and wickedness. A reminder of *why* the earth had been overcome by a flood in the first place.

"*Ach*, did you find something over there?" Martha rounded the corner.

"Uh." He quickly grabbed the woodworking magazine not far from the one he'd been gazing at with the bodybuilding image. He showed her the cover with a children's playset on it. "Been thinking of trying out some projects."

Liar.

"*Ach*, really? I didn't know you were interested in building things."

He caught the amazement in her voice. If only he could be the man she thought he was.

"Just thinking about it, is all." He shrugged.

"Have you ever built anything like that?"

"*Nee.*" He chastised himself.

"Should we go now? We don't want the ice cream to melt." She stared at him. "Are you going to buy that?"

"Uh, *jah*." He quickly stuck the magazine in the shopping cart. "Let's go home."

Aside from the unwelcome looks he'd received from Nathaniel, the evening had gone *wunderbaar*. He hated bidding Martha farewell, not knowing when he'd see her again. No doubt, they'd both be really busy this next week, so he likely wouldn't see her till the following week. If he could stand to wait that long.

Martha had walked out to the phone shanty with him to call his driver. He hung up the phone, then pulled her into his arms.

"I'm going to miss you like crazy next week." He bent down and met her lips.

"It will go by fast." She closed her eyes and leaned in to his chest.

He held her tight and sighed deeply. "I hope so."

A knock on the phone shanty door forced him to release her and put proper distance between them. Not that it was an easy feat inside a small phone booth.

He yanked the door open.

"Nathaniel? What are you doing out here?" Martha frowned at her *bruder*.

"I need to talk to Jaden before he leaves."

Jaden groaned inwardly.

"Okay," Martha said.

"Go on back to the house, Martha," her *bruder* commanded. "It's him I want to talk to."

Martha eyed him, a frown etched on her face.

Jaden swallowed. "It's okay, Martha. We won't be long." He angled his head toward the house.

Martha's gaze ping-ponged between the two men. She shrugged. "Fine."

Both men watched her until she had entered the house.

TWENTY-ONE

"*Y*ou are going to break up with *mei schweschder.*" Nathaniel's words hadn't been a request, but a command. *Nee*, a demand.

"No, I'm not."

"Fine. Have it your way." Nathaniel turned and began walking toward the house.

"What are you doing?" Jaden hollered after him.

"I'm going to march back into the house and tell *everyone* the truth about who you are."

Ach, he *really* did not like this guy.

"Wait!" Jaden grabbed hold of Nathaniel's arm.

"Get your hand off my body!"

Jaden muted the curse word interlaced with Nathaniel's speech, then released his grip. "Don't say anything. *Please*." *Ach*, he hated the desperation in his voice.

"There is only *one* way you will get me to keep my

mouth closed. There will be no negotiation." Nathaniel insisted. "Walk away from my *schweschder* and from my family."

Even more than the anger that surged through Jaden's veins, sorrow clenched his heart as he considered Nathaniel's words. Life would feel so empty without his beloved Martha in it. "I don't know if I can do that."

"You *can* and you *will*."

Jaden squeezed his eyes shut.

An *Englisch* vehicle pulled in, and Jaden waved to the driver.

"It's simple. Get in that car and don't come back. Don't call *mei schweschder* or write her any letters. You need to disappear from her life entirely."

"But she would be devastated." *He* would be devastated.

"More than finding out the truth? Trust me, she'll move on without you. She'll get over it." Nathaniel smirked. "I hear Titus Troyer already has his eye on her."

Ach. Jaden swallowed. His heart felt like it might stop. He had no choice but to agree to Nathaniel's demands. But the more he thought about it, the more he agreed with Martha's *bruder*. She was better off without him.

"Fine." Jaden swirled around and headed straight to the car.

He never deserved Martha anyhow.

As his driver headed toward Josiah's place, Jaden kept his face toward the passenger side window. He wouldn't let him see the tears that trailed his cheeks. He wouldn't allow this *Englisch* stranger to be privy to his sanctuary of grief.

Martha frowned when Nathaniel returned to the house alone. "Where's Jaden?"

"*Ach.*" Nathaniel shrugged. "He had to go. His driver showed up."

"He isn't even going to say goodbye?" She hurried to look out the window, only to see a vehicle's taillights heading down the road.

"Guess not."

She watched her *bruder* take the stairs two at a time.

Martha puzzled over Jaden's actions. He'd never left without saying goodbye. Had something gone wrong?

TWENTY-TWO

Martha stared at the school calendar. It was Friday already. The last day of the scholars' school year. The week had gone smoothly, but she'd been surprised Jaden hadn't called. She'd thought about him all week and wondered how his new job was going. How had he adjusted to the new school? Did he get along with the teacher? Did the scholars like him?

She supposed he was probably busy. Had he thought about her during the week? Wondered how she was doing? It was a strange thing to spend every day of one week with someone, then not hear so much as a peep from them the week after. Especially when those two someones were in love.

She would stop at the shanty and give him a call as soon as she returned home. She could leave a message, then ask him to call back at a certain time.

❧

"Jaden, there was a message for you at the phone shanty." Josiah stuck his hat on the hall tree just inside the house.

"Who was it from? What did it say?"

"Martha Miller. She asked for you to call her back at seven tonight."

Jaden grunted.

"What's wrong? I thought you were courting her."

"*Nee.*"

"What?"

"Not anymore."

"She broke up with you? Is that why you didn't join the men's fellowship last week?"

That, and he seemed to be failing at everything in life. "Something like that."

"You know, I find the times I try to skip out on fellowship are the times that I need it most."

Jaden knew his brother was right.

"Sammy asked how you were doing. I said you were fine. But I'm not sure that was the most accurate answer." Josiah studied him. "Are you coming tomorrow?"

Jaden shrugged.

"What is going on with you?"

"I'm thinking of moving back to Pennsylvania."

"What? Why? What about your teaching job? I put in a good word for you."

He covered his face with his hand. "I know." He moaned.

"Are you running away from something? Someone? It isn't like you to not keep your word."

"Do you ever feel like life would be easier if you just went away? Disappeared and went somewhere else where nobody knew you?"

"Jaden. *Hello*. It's *me* you're talking to. Your brother, Josiah, who did *exactly* that."

Jaden frowned.

"Look where I am today. Yeah, I'm fine *now*. But I missed out on being a part of most of my daughter's life. I missed out on almost two decades with our family. Those are years I can never get back again. So, do I regret it? You bet I do. If I had the chance to go back, would I do it again? No, I would not. But God dug me out of the mess I'd made and helped me to salvage those relationships, then blessed me with new ones."

"I don't know how to fix the messes I've made."

Josiah squeezed his shoulder. "Then let go, and let God."

Jaden pondered the wisdom of his *bruder's* words.

Josiah chuckled. "I've always wanted to use that cliché. But seriously. Pray about it and ask God to direct your path. He will."

Jaden sighed. "Is life *ever* easy?"

"Is that what you want? Easy? Nothing comes easy. Especially relationships. If you want something, you have to work at it. God gives us the building materials, but it's up to us to make something out of them. We can leave them there and do nothing with them until they disintegrate into a pile of dust. Or we can grab a hammer and nails and build a palace to live in or a boat to sail around the world in."

"You talk like an *Englischer.*"

Josiah tapped the side of his head. "That's hard-earned wisdom right there."

Jaden chuckled. "Is that what you call it?"

His *bruder* smiled. "Something like that."

Martha sat out in the phone shanty at ten till seven, then waited until seven fifteen before picking up the phone to dial Jaden's number again. Why hadn't he called? Had he been busy?

"Hello, Jaden. It's Martha Miller again. Um...if you could just call back whenever and leave a message telling me when a good time is to call you back, that would be *gut*." She left her number in case he'd lost or forgotten it, then hung up the phone.

She sighed. "What's going on with you, Jaden?"

TWENTY-THREE

"I'm glad you came to see me. I've been worried about you."

Ach, just being in Sammy's presence caused a peace to wash over Jaden. He didn't know what it was about this man, but there was definitely something special.

"I hoped you'd show up tomorrow morning." The older man said. "But today is fine too."

"I'm a mess, Sammy." He admitted.

"Wanna tell me about it?"

Jaden glanced around the barn. "Is anyone here?"

"I suppose everyone's out and about." He gestured to his horse. "Why don't we take a ride in my buggy? No interruptions there."

"Okay." He helped Sammy hitch up the horse.

"You talk. I'll drive." Sammy motioned for him to enter the passenger's side."

As soon as the buggy wheels hit the pavement, Jaden gave Sammy a rundown of the past week and a half, leaving out very few details.

"It doesn't sound all bad. Both of your teaching projects went well, then?" Sammy's brow arched.

"They did."

"Have you been reading your Bible every day?"

"I'm afraid I've failed in that area."

"I see." Sammy nodded. "Well, that explains a lot. *Walk in the Spirit and ye shall not fulfill the lusts of the flesh.* Whenever we walk in the flesh, we're destined for failure. God's words must be our sustenance."

"I do still have a couple of verses memorized and they have helped me. Especially the imagination one."

Sammy frowned, a question in his eyes.

"Casting down imaginations." Jaden reminded him.

"That's a *gut* one, for sure."

"It helps me when wicked thoughts pop into my mind."

"The key is to not dwell on evil when we see it. Job said, "I will set no wicked thing before mine eyes." It is not that we will never see things. We will. But the key is to not allow our mind to dwell on these things. It all goes back to submitting our thoughts to *Der*

Herr and casting down imaginations, like you mentioned.

"Remember what we read? *Resist the devil and he will flee from you*. You *must* resist. If you don't, then you are inviting him to wreak havoc in your life. I don't think you want that. *Resist the devil, draw nigh to Gott*. That is the only way to get victory over sin. You *must* resist. You *must* cling to *Der Herr*. And it is difficult to do that when you are not in His Word every day."

Jaden took a breath and nodded. "What should I do about Martha, then?"

"You could try being honest with her. She deserves to know the truth."

"*Ach*, that would be hard."

"*Jah*, but you've already deserted her for less than that. You can't live your life in fear. If you do, you'll always be running. You'll never have rest for your soul."

"And what about her *bruder* Nathaniel?"

"There's a *gut* chance his view will change once you've been honest and you and Martha have worked things out." Sammy eyed him, then trained his gaze back on the road. "You say he's going on that mission trip?"

Jaden nodded.

"That sounds like a *gut* opportunity to lay things out for Martha. But I also think you need to be honest with the guys. You need them on your side. You need their prayers and support. We are all in this together. Remember, none of us is without sin. *He that covereth his sins shall not prosper: but whoso confesseth and forsaketh them shall find mercy.*

"The steps of a good man are ordered by the Lord: and He delighteth in his way. Though he fall, he shall not be utterly cast down: for the Lord upholdeth him with His hand. Der Herr is on your side, *sohn.* It is impossible to fail when you follow His lead."

"Do you think I should share things with the guys tomorrow, then?" Jaden held his breath.

"That's a *gut* place to start. I will be praying for you."

Jaden didn't think he'd ever been more nervous in this life. Even now, the cup of coffee trembled in his hands. *Ach*, how could he do this?

Gott, please give me the strength.

All the men gathered around the living room, and as they always did, Sammy led off with prayer.

"Before we begin, Jaden has a confession he'd like to make." Sammy nodded for Jaden to share his heart.

He took a deep breath. *Ach*, this was hard. But he respected and trusted these men. "I'm overcoming homosexuality."

Jaden didn't miss Silas's eyes widening or Paul's jaw dropping. Michael nodded. Josiah frowned.

He forged on. "I'm not going to lie. Part of me wants to run with the world that accepts every behavior and says everything is permissible. But I've given my life to *Gott* and I want to be pleasing to Him. Sammy showed me that the only way to overcome sin is to confess it and forsake it. That is my struggle. And if you guys could help me and keep me in your prayers, I would be grateful. Because it *is* a struggle. But by *Gott's* grace, I know I can overcome it."

Sammy looked at each of the men and encouraged them to lay their hands on Jaden and say a prayer for him. Jaden didn't know if it was his own emotions or the power of the Holy Spirit in the room, but the presence of *Gott* felt so real. It was almost like a hug from *Der Herr*, and it brought him to tears.

When the men finished praying, Jaden knew the power of *Gott* had touched them too. His *bruder* engulfed him in a bear hug and told him that he was proud of him for coming forward. Now that he knew what Jaden was dealing with, he'd know better how to pray for him and how to help him. The men also pledged to help hold him accountable. Even Martha's older brothers were encouraging.

Jaden never knew what it was like to have friends like this. This was how he pictured the family of *Gott* to be. And he was so glad to be a part of it. But he needed to remind himself that he wasn't the only one with struggles. These men needed his prayers as much as he needed theirs.

TWENTY-FOUR

$\int$aden smiled as some of the scholars came up to greet him after the church meeting. He had apparently made many friends during his teaching stint last week. Several of the parents regarded him kindly, as well.

He glanced toward the house to see if there was any movement yet. The non-members had been asked to step out while the members had a meeting. Everyone knew what the meeting was about.

Ten minutes later, people began filing outside the house and Jaden helped the men set up the tables and benches for the common meal. He glanced around for his *bruder*, then finally spotted him toward the back of the group still exiting the house.

The women moved about, setting out place settings and dishes of food on each table. But Jaden couldn't think of eating at the moment. He needed to know the outcome of the meeting. Finding out what had transpired would require him to sequester his *bruder* or Sammy away from the others. He couldn't wait until the buggy ride back to Josiah's house. He needed to know now.

He pulled his *bruder* aside. Josiah hadn't said a word, but the apologetic look he'd given Jaden said it all. Detweiler's district had chosen to disfellowship with Bontrager's.

Ach, this couldn't be happening.

Jaden glanced out the side of the buggy, lost in thought as his *bruder* drove toward home.

"It isn't all bad news, though. Family members in the districts can still fellowship. So Bailey is free to come and go," Josiah said.

"*Jah*, but what about the *youngie*?"

"That's the bad news. No dating between the church districts. I'm sorry, *bruder*. I wish the news were better."

"What about our men's group?"

Josiah shrugged. "That's pretty much been covert from the start. The leaders know nothing about it."

"So, Sammy won't uphold the *Bann*?"

"As far as I know, Sammy's always pretty much

done his own thing. I don't doubt he'd risk shunning over it. He's more inclined to let *Gott* lead him on such matters."

It looked like another trip to Sammy's was in order. He needed some advice.

"I'm afraid I can't tell you what to do in this matter," Sammy said. "You have to obey your conscience and only *you* know what it is telling you. Just make sure it is your conscience—or the nudging of the Spirit—and *not* your heart. Remember, *the heart is deceitful above all things and desperately wicked*. The faith of many has been derailed because they've followed their hearts. You pray about it, then let *Der Herr* guide you. I will be praying for you too."

Jaden blew out a breath. "*Denki*, Sammy."

"Do you know what time the mission group is heading out tomorrow?" Jaden asked Josiah over supper.

"First thing in the morning." He took a bite of his fried chicken. "Bailey is still stewing over it."

"She really wanted to go." Nora commented. Jaden caught the sympathy in his sister-in-law's voice.

Josiah sighed. "I know. But, honestly, I'm siding

with Timothy on this one. It isn't safe for her to travel right now."

"I suppose she'll eventually get over it," Nora said.

"As soon as she has her *boppli*, she'll realize it was worth it." Josiah smiled. "Nothing like holding your own flesh and blood in your arms for the first time. Right, *fraa*?"

"True." She nodded.

"I still can't believe I'm going to be a *grossdawdi*." Josiah shook his head.

"It's pretty crazy. I'll have to call you an old man now." Jaden teased.

TWENTY-FIVE

*J*aden waited until an hour past the time Josiah had said the mission group would leave, before calling his driver. He couldn't chance running into Nathaniel, not until he explained everything to Martha.

Even though he wasn't allowed to date her, he needed to let her know what was going on. Who knew? There was a *gut* chance she wouldn't want to have anything to do with him once she found out the truth. All he knew was that he had to explain things from his point of view before she heard rumors from anywhere else.

He'd been praying all morning for the right words and that *Der Herr* would give Martha an understanding heart.

As soon as the car rolled to a stop, he handed over the money and slid out. He hoped Martha was home.

Just in case, he'd asked his driver to wait.

He bounced on his toes as he knocked on the door. When Martha opened it, he quickly dismissed his driver.

"Jaden! You're here."

Ach, her smile was the most beautiful thing he'd ever seen. He would have taken her in his arms then and there, if he hadn't heard one of her family members shuffling around in the kitchen.

She stared at him. "How come you didn't return my phone calls?"

"It's a long story. Do you have time to talk right now?"

"*Ach*, I was just about to take the wash out to hang up. You can help me."

"You got it." He stepped into the house and hefted the basket laden with wet clothing. "Lead the way, *schatzi*."

"You know *mei bruder* and *schweschder* left this morning, right?" She walked out to the clothesline that stretched from the barn to another outbuilding.

He nodded.

She bent down and picked up one of the wet dresses.

Jaden helped by pinning it to the line. "Did you hear the news yet?"

"What news?"

"Detweiler's had a meeting yesterday." Heaviness pressed in as he said the words.

"And?"

"No dating between districts." His eyes sought hers.

"*Ach, nee*!"

"So, if we're going to court, it will have to be in secret."

"But we already are."

He reached over and slid his hand across hers. "I know. But I'm still in my proving time. I have three weeks yet before they'll count me as a member."

"Do we have to stop seeing each other then?"

"Trying to keep me away from the most beautiful girl in the world is like trying to keep hungry ants away from a summer picnic." He pulled her by the hand until they were behind the barn and out of sight of the house and road. He trapped her between himself and the barn, a hand on the siding near each of her shoulders. He bent down, dropping his lips to hers, and her arms laced around his neck, pressing her form against him. "*Ach*, Martha."

He couldn't let himself get carried away. Not when he hadn't shared the truth with her yet.

"We need to talk," he murmured in her ear. "Let's

finish the laundry before your *mamm* or *schweschder* comes out."

Her hand slid up his chest, tempting him further. "If we have to."

He caught the desire in her eyes.

"*Schatzi.*" He groaned, then brought her close, tasting her lips once again. Did they really *have* to talk right now? Because he *really* didn't care to.

"Uh...hum!" A throat cleared behind them.

Jaden and Martha instantly broke apart but his heart continued to race frantically.

"Emily!" Martha grunted.

"I thought that was what you two might be doing out here." She thrust a hand on her hip. "Martha, laundry needs done."

"Don't say anything to *Mamm*, okay?" Martha said, sharing a worried glance with Jaden.

"Whatever." Martha's youngest sister rolled her eyes.

"I mean it. Jaden's not even supposed to be here. Detweiler's shunned us."

Emily gasped. "What?" She looked to Jaden for confirmation.

He nodded. "It's true."

"What are you guys going to do?"

Jaden felt like saying *I thought that was obvious*, but decided against it.

"Well, we're going to do laundry right now," Martha said.

"Uh-huh." Emily shook her head, then prodded back toward the house. She called over her shoulder. "I'm going to be watching you two!"

Martha giggled. "Well, I guess we better put this laundry up. What was that you wanted to say?"

"*Ach*, I'll tell you later."

"*Nee*, tell me now. I don't like waiting."

"Martha." He sighed heavily. "You're not going to like what I have to say."

She stopped what she was doing and stared at him. "Why?"

"Remember how I told you about my past and that I'd learned things I wish I hadn't, and did things that I wasn't proud of?"

"*Jah*."

"Well, I still struggle with those issues."

"What issues?"

He looked around. It wouldn't do if her *schweschder* Emily was somewhere listening in on their conversation. He moved close and whispered his secrets in her ear.

Martha gasped, then frowned. "Jaden." She stepped back—away from him.

He tried not to take it as a rejection. He wasn't sure

he could stand rejection from the woman he'd come to love more than anything. He sucked in a breath and held it.

It took her a moment to find words. "I don't know what to say. What am I supposed to do with that?"

"If it makes you feel any better, I'm doing my best to put it behind me. But I knew I needed to be honest with you. That is what I struggle with."

"So, what does that mean for us?" Tears shimmered in her eyes. "Do you not find me attractive?"

"*Ach*, Martha. You already know that I do." He frowned. His voice lowered. "Have you already forgotten last Sunday?"

"*Nee*, I could never ever forget that." Her cheeks darkened, then the corner of her lips turned down. "It's just...if you're enticed by *that*, I don't know if I'll be able to trust you. Because you will be among other men every time you are away from me."

"I know. I realize that. But everyone that I know of around here isn't the same way I am."

"But what if someone was? And they befriended you? And you were attracted to them?" Tears welled in her eyes. "Jaden, I just couldn't. I couldn't be married to you and be wondering if my husband is..."

"If we marry, I will be fully committed to *us* and our family, if *Der Herr* blesses us with one."

"I don't know if that's enough." She sobbed.

He refrained from taking her into his arms. "All I can do is my best. I can't pledge a perfect sinless life. It doesn't exist for *any* of us. I'm afraid that's all I can promise you, Martha. "I would understand if you wanted to end our relationship." He swallowed, hoping—*praying*—she wouldn't. "Right now."

"Is that what you want?"

"*Nee*, not at all. I love you, *schatzi*." He swallowed, hating the fact that this was hurting her. "Here's the thing, though. I've asked *Der Herr* to help me, and I really think He is. The Bible says that if we delight in *Gott* then He will give us the desires of our hearts. I understand that to mean that He will put the desires He wants us to have into our hearts. I feel like that is what He is doing with me. Because I've never wanted a relationship with someone as much as I do with you. I've fallen in love with you, Martha Miller. And, by the grace of *Gott*, I want to spend all my days with you. I will do my best to do right by you.

"But I cannot promise you perfection. Sammy said that if I stay near to *Gott*, then He will stay close to me. I am trying to do that. I'm trying to let *Der Herr* lead me. I have several people praying for me about this."

"*Other* people know about this?"

"Some do, *jah*. Silas and Paul both promised to

pray for me, as I have for them. Also, my *bruder* Josiah, and Sammy and Michael. All of them have agreed to help keep me accountable. I don't want to have any more regrets. I want to live a life that is pleasing to *Der Herr*."

"But you are going against the *Ordnung* by being here. By being with me, ain't not?"

"*Ach*, I know."

"It is not pleasing to *Der Herr* to go against your authority." She frowned. "I don't want to be the one who comes between you and *Gott*, Jaden. I won't be that person. Besides, we've already gotten too involved."

"What are you saying?" His brow furrowed.

"I don't know. Maybe we should take a break for a while. You have your proving time yet. How long has it been since you were with the other people?" She swallowed.

He could tell she hated asking the question. But she deserved to know. "About five or six years. If it makes you feel better, I can get tested to make sure I don't have any diseases."

"It would make me feel a little better." She nodded. "But I think I need time to process this and pray about it. I really don't know how much time I'll need."

"But you're not going to let Titus Troyer court you, ain't not?"

Martha sighed. "Jaden, how many times do I have to tell you that I have no interest in Titus Troyer? You can put that thought out of your head now."

"So...you want to *just* pray?" His frown deepened. "You're not breaking up with me forever, are you?"

"Jaden Beachy. Stop, already. Look, I'm still going to be here. I'm not going anywhere. But I want *you* to be sure. You need to spend more time with Michael's *grossdawdi*, I think. And I don't want you to lose your job. You should be a school teacher. All the *kinner* love you."

"But what about us?"

"We're waiting and praying, remember? And absence is supposed to make the heart grow fonder."

"Praying. Right." He shook his head. "Martha, I honestly don't know if I'll be able to stay away from you."

"If you need a kiss, you can just come and get one. In secret."

"So, you're *not* breaking up with me then?"

"Jaden Beachy! Did you hear any of what I just said?" She thrust her hand on her hip, clearly put out with him. "Listen very closely. I. Love. You. I. Still. Want. To. Marry. You. Understand?"

"*Jah*. But when?"

Her smile returned. "It is not my place to do the

asking or the telling. You know that."

"In the fall, then? Next wedding season?" He couldn't hide his goofy grin.

"Let's see if we think we're ready by then."

"I hope we are."

"I'm a little scared, Jaden. If you want to know the truth."

He took her hands in his, his thumbs lightly caressing her soft veins. "I know you are. The unknown is always scary. I'm not sure what more I can do to assure you."

"I think it is something *Der Herr* will have to place in my heart. I need peace."

"All I know is that *Gott* will be with us every step of the way, no matter what happens."

"That is something."

"*Nee*, that is *everything*, Martha." He needed to pray that she could see that clearly.

"*Jah*, you're right."

TWENTY-SIX

Jaden hadn't expected to return home to the deacon's buggy in his *bruder's* driveway. *Ach*, a visit with the deacon usually meant something was wrong or there'd been an infraction regarding the *Ordnung*. Had his *bruder* done something worthy of the deacon's visit? Had the leaders learned of their clandestine Bible studies?

He was tempted to hang out outside, after putting up his *bruder's* horse, until the deacon left. But that action might be frowned upon. He didn't want the deacon to think he was hiding out or anything.

"Jaden Beachy." The deacon nodded and shook his hand as soon as he'd walked through the door. "Just the man I wanted to see. May we chat outside?"

Jaden frowned, then glanced at his *bruder*, quirking a brow. Josiah shrugged in return, nodding for him to comply with the deacon's wishes.

Jaden followed the man outside.

"The leaders asked me to stop by each home in our district to better explain the new changes to the Ordnung."

Jaden nodded, but held his breath.

"Some have said you are courting a *maedel* from Bontrager's district. Is this true?"

"It is." He wouldn't deny it.

"Are you aware that the new changes forbid the two churches to intermingle?"

"What are you saying?"

"You must cut ties with this *maedel*."

"But we are engaged."

"The wedding season isn't until fall. Nothing has been published."

"*Nee*, but we've discussed it between ourselves."

"No matter. I'm sorry. I do not make the rules, I'm *chust* in charge of enforcing them." The deacon's gaze held sympathy, but his stance was unyielding. "If it makes you feel better, you are not the only one to have to break things off. There are others who have been courting longer than you have been here. Be grateful you are not one of them.

"The leaders will be watching closely to be sure the *Ordnung* is kept. Since you are in the time of proving, I'm afraid it will be even more so with you." The deacon tipped his hat, headed toward his buggy, then set off down the road.

Jaden stood open-mouthed as he watched the deacon's buggy disappear around the corner. *Ach*, he'd need to call Martha. But he had no idea what he would say. They'd already agreed—for the most part, anyhow—to not see each other until his proving was over. But what would happen after that? Would they continue to sneak around even though the *Ordnung* forbid it? And then what? They still planned to marry in the fall. They could marry in her district, but that would mean he'd likely lose his job and be shunned.

He thought on Martha's words. *We will pray. Nee*, he wouldn't call Martha. Why add more worry upon her shoulders? They had already expected as much. For now, they would wait and pray like they'd agreed to do.

In spite of her previous hesitation, Martha's heart couldn't help but overflow with joy. *Ach*, she and Jaden could be getting hitched this year! But as excited as she was, it seemed *Mamm* was even more so. As a matter of fact, they'd been working in the garden the last couple of days, preparing the ground for a *gut* celery harvest. Now was a *gut* time to start planting, if the plants were to be ready in the fall. If they decided against a wedding, they could always sell off the extra celery at Emily's produce stand.

She still wasn't sure how everything would work itself out. She'd been diligent in praying for Jaden and his struggles. The secrets he'd shared with her had been alarming, she admitted. But then it was almost like someone had whispered in her ear and told her everything would be okay. Had it been the voice of *Der Herr*? She didn't know.

But she *did* know that their love for each other was strong. She wasn't so naïve as to think they would never have struggles or they'd get along seamlessly. Every marriage took work. And even though her and Jaden's situation was different, she was determined to stand beside him, support him, and pray for him.

And being as it was, she knew that, with *Der Herr* on their side, everything would work out. It had to.

TWENTY-SEVEN

*F*or the weeks apart from Martha, Jaden had begun pouring himself into the portions of the Bible that Sammy had recommended to him. He loved that Sammy was in the same *g'may* and lived within walking distance of his *bruder's* house. If Jaden had a question, he would just jump on one of his *bruder's* horses and head down the road to see Sammy.

His faith grew stronger every day, and the temptations lessened. *Der Herr* had been faithful in fulfilling His promises of resisting the devil and drawing nigh unto Him. He loved having a faith that was real and measurable. He loved that *Gott* encouraged His children to prove Himself.

He and Martha had agreed to keep in touch over the phone while he was going through his proving. Hearing her voice helped him stay grounded in their relationship, although their calls weren't daily. It had been a few days now since hearing her voice, and he missed her.

Just as he'd been preparing to dial her number, the phone rang.

"Hello?" He spoke into the receiver.

"Jaden? Is that you?" Martha's voice sounded shaky, off.

"Martha? Are you crying? *Was itz lets, lieb*?"

"I need you to come over. Can you do that?"

"*Ach*, of course. I'll call a driver right now."

"*Denki.*"

The phone clicked off.

Jaden worried the entire car ride over. What could be wrong? Had someone fallen sick or gotten injured on the mission trip? Was the family okay? A hundred different scenarios played through his head, but none of them prepared him for *this*.

She handed him a small white plastic device that reminded him of his *mamm's* digital thermometer, but there were no numbers on it.

He stared at the thing, completely puzzled. He shrugged. "What is it?"

"What do you see?" She swiped away a tear.

"Just two blue lines." He stared at her. "What does it mean?"

"I've been sick for the last three days. *Mamm* asked about us, and I told her the truth about what we did."

He stared at her. Blinked. What was she trying to tell him?

"Jaden, I'm in the *familye* way." A fresh crop of tears surfaced on her eyelashes.

"You're…" He swallowed. "Martha? Is this…this is for real? We are going to have a *boppli*?"

"*Jah.*" She heaved a sob.

A *boppli*? He thought on it for a minute. This meant they *had to* get hitched now. *Nee*, they couldn't have a normal wedding, but…

"*Ach*, this is the answer to our prayers!" Even though he *should* feel guilty, excitement bubbled in his chest.

"What?" She sniffled.

"Think about it, Martha. I didn't tell you this, but the deacon came by two weeks ago and told me that I had to break our engagement. We wouldn't have been allowed to marry. But now, we will *have* to."

"You act as though it is a *gut* thing. It is not. We should have waited to share the marriage bed till we got hitched."

He took her hands in his, offering an encouraging

smile. "*Ach*, Martha. A *boppli* is always a *gut* thing. *Nee*, we didn't go about things the right way. But we will make things right."

"But what will we do?" She stared at him. "We won't be able to hide it from the *g'may*."

"We will go talk to Sammy. He always has the answer."

Sammy rubbed his beard, his gaze pinning Jaden. "*Ach*, I do not remember you confessing *this* sin. You have been hiding things."

"I'm sorry, Sammy. Since I'm confessing, I might as well tell you that it happened on *Der Herr's* day too. My sins are many, I'm afraid." Jaden sighed, then reached over and squeezed Martha's hand. "We have already repented before *Der Herr* and have decided to stay pure till we get hitched."

Sammy eyed Martha for confirmation. "This is true? Not that I don't trust Jaden."

Martha nodded, her cheeks ablaze with color.

"What do you think will happen as far as the leaders go?" Jaden queried.

"My guess is the same as it was with Michael and Miriam. You will have to go to the justice of the peace. Likely tomorrow."

Martha gasped and Jaden's eyes widened.

"*Tomorrow?*" They both asked in unison.

Sammy nodded. "Then you'll be in the *Bann* for another six weeks. I'm not sure what will happen with your job."

Martha squeezed Jaden's hand, proffering reassurance. "There are other jobs, ain't not?"

"Right." Jaden scratched his cheek. "I'll also need to start looking for a place of our own. We can stay with my *bruder* now, I know he won't mind, but we will want to be on our own before the *boppli* comes."

Sammy nodded. "That's a gut idea. And if you think about it, it's not *all* bad. Since Martha is Silas and Paul's *schweschder*, you will now be related to them. According to the new rules of the *Ordnung*, that opens the door of fellowship."

"So *Der Herr* truly did work this out for us." Jaden's smile broadened.

"*Jah*, He did. *All things work together for* gut, *for those that love* Gott *and are the called according to His purpose*." Sammy shook his finger at Jaden. "But that does *not* mean He is condoning your sin. *Chust* because *Der Herr* makes a message out of our mess, does not mean our messes are a *gut* thing. It *chust* means we have a *gut Gott*."

"Do we ever." Jaden grinned.

"For certain." Sammy's eyes connected with

Jaden's. "He who has been forgiven much, loves much. I think this applies to you, *sohn*. *Der Herr* will do many *gut* works through your life, if you allow Him to."

Tears pricked Martha's eyes as she stood in front of the justice of the peace, holding hands with her beloved. She glanced behind them and smiled at those who had come out to celebrate their union as husband and wife. *Mamm* and *Dat*, Jaden's *bruder* Josiah and his *fraa* Nora, her *breider* Silas and Paul and their *fraas* Kayla and Jenny, her *schweschder* Emily, their niece Bailey and her husband Timothy, and Jaden's *gut* friend Sammy and his *gross sohn* Michael with his *fraa* Miriam. Her best friend Amy stood as her witness, as did Josiah for Jaden.

In spite of all that had happened with the leaders, gladness filled her heart. At her age, she didn't care for a big fancy Amish wedding. This simple *Englisch* wedding, surrounded by those she loved, felt absolutely perfect. *Nee*, it wasn't exactly how she'd envisioned it. But *Der Herr* had seen fit to bless her beyond measure anyhow. He'd fulfilled the longing of her heart.

She had *everything* that mattered—the sweetest

husband in the whole world, whose *boppli* she now carried, the support of those who loved her most, and a *Gott* she'd begun a brand-new relationship with just yesterday. She couldn't wait to see what the future held, but she knew that whatever transpired, *Der Herr* would be with them through all of it.

And His love was more than she could ever ask for.

EPILOGUE

*A*s Jaden held a brand new *boppli* in each of his arms, he couldn't help think of the verse he'd read and pondered over that morning. *Many are the afflictions of the righteous, but the Lord delivereth him out of them all.* And *Der Herr* had. No matter what the devil had placed in Jaden's path to try to trip him up, he'd clung to *Der Herr* and found victory.

Not that he was never tempted or fell or had achieved perfection. Far from it. But when he *did* fall, *Der Herr* was waiting on the sidelines with open arms to help dust off his knees and get back into the race. He found that having a *fraa* helped greatly with temptation and the sins of his past. *Der Herr* had replaced his old sinful desires with new desires that brought glory to *Gott*.

"Are you going to hold them all day or do I get to

see our *sohn* and *dochder*?" Martha teased.

Jaden stared down into the innocent eyes of the precious lives *Gott* had created through them. He still couldn't get over *Gott's* goodness to him. "*Kumm,* little ones, your mama wants to hold you."

"Their *aentis* and *onkels* will be arriving soon, so I want to hold them all I can." His *fraa* smiled as Jaden reluctantly handed over their adorable *bopplin*.

Thinking of aunts and uncles...needless to say, Susan and Nathaniel returning home from their mission trip to find Jaden and Martha hitched and expecting a *boppli*, had been nothing less than shocking.

Equally shocking was the day Nathaniel had showed up to their men's fellowship. Jaden thought on it now...

"Let's welcome Silas and Paul's brother Nathaniel to our group," Sammy had said.

They'd each shaken his hand, but Nathaniel frowned when he saw Jaden. "Is *he* part of this group too?"

Sammy looked back and forth between Nathaniel and Jaden, seeming to sum up the situation. "We're all sinners saved by grace, here. If you are not a sinner, maybe this isn't the group for you." Sammy's gaze pierced Nathaniel.

Nathaniel had acquiesced and by the end of their

meeting, Jaden and Nathaniel had come to an understanding and a friendship of sorts. Now, it seemed Nathaniel hardly remembered Jaden's past failures.

"It's too bad you have to go back to work tomorrow. It's so soon." Martha's words yanked him from his musings and her frown propelled him toward her.

He bent down and kissed her forehead. "The scholars need me there. You will have your *schweschdern* Emily and Susan here to help with whatever you need. Besides, I'll be home by four. The life of a teacher may be demanding, but the hours are *gut*."

"*Jah.* I do miss it sometimes."

"You won't be missing anything now that we have these *bopplin*, I assure you. They will keep you busy, no doubt. I just hope we can be *gut* teachers for these little ones."

"I think that as long as we point them to Jesus— the ultimate teacher—they will do fine." She caressed the *bopplin's* fine hair.

Jaden leaned down and kissed Martha's lips. "You're right *fraa*. You are absolutely right."

THE END

Dear Reader,

I hope you enjoyed Jaden and Martha's story! *Jah*, it was different.

Wow, what a difficult subject to tackle. Our society has changed so much in the last few decades. Sometimes, it is hard to know what to do or where to stand, especially when cultural norms conflict with our conscience.

Things that the majority of society once felt were wrong are now labeled right. If you stand for the Truth, persecution is almost a guarantee. What's a Christian to do?

Let me just say that **God and His Word are unchanging**.

God's Word says in Isaiah 5:20, *"Woe unto them that call evil good, and good evil; that put darkness for light, and light for darkness; that put bitter for sweet, and sweet for bitter!"*

As the world grows darker, we *must* shine brighter. We must not compromise. We know Who wins the battle in the end.

In light of this book's subject, I'd like to recommend a resource that I have found valuable. It's a book by Joe Dallas called *When Homosexuality Hits Home (What to do when a loved one says, "I'm gay").* The author, Joe Dallas, has been on both sides of the issue in a very real way. He tackles issues/circumstances that will help every Christian, I believe.

I also encourage you to read the book of Romans (Holy Bible, KJV), as it is, as Sammy said, "Chock-full of *gut* stuff."

Remember above all, **God is love**. He accepts us just the way we are, but He loves us too much to leave us that way. Do you recall what Jesus said to the woman caught in adultery? He didn't condone her sin, but demonstrated what love looks like. He said, *"Neither do I condemn thee: go, and sin no more."*

Let's stand firm in these last days.

I'll leave you with this verse from First Corinthians 15:58. *"Therefore, my beloved brethren, be ye stedfast, unmoveable, always abounding in the work of the Lord, forasmuch as ye know that your labour is not in vain in the Lord."*

Blessings in Christ,
Jennifer Spredemann

Thanks for reading!
Word of mouth is one of the best forms of
advertisement and a HUGE blessing to the
author. If you enjoyed this book, **please** consider
leaving a review, sharing on social media, and
telling your reading friends.

THANK YOU!

GET THE NEXT BOOK...

The Widower (Amish Country Brides)

Emily Miller loves tending her garden and roadside stand, but she admits her love life is dull. While she's ridden home from singings with several young men from her community, none of them fulfills the image her mind's eye conjures up. She wants a man who is not only kind and hardworking, but responsible and loves children. So, when shy widower Titus Troyer shows up at her roadside stand with his adorable *kinner*, something tugs at her heart.

Titus Troyer made a fool out of himself when he prematurely asked Martha Miller to marry him and attempted a courtship with her, and he doesn't intend to ever repeat that mistake. But when vibrant Emily Miller, Martha's younger sister, meets his eye at her family's roadside stand, he can't deny his attraction. But would a pretty, and very available, young woman like Emily even give a man like him a second thought? More importantly, can he summon the courage to find out?

A sweet love story about finding love when you least expect it.

DISCUSSION QUESTIONS

1. Martha Miller and Jaden Beachy have a friendship through letter writing. Have you ever had a pen pal? If so, how long did the letter-writing relationship last?

2. Have you ever been a party to a long-distance relationship?

3. Martha enjoys baking her delicious coffee cake. Do you have a favorite recipe? Does it hold special significance?

4. Jaden is excited to move and begin a new job. Have you ever had to relocate for a job?

5. Have you ever had a surprise visit from a friend or loved one?

6. Jaden is fearful to share his secret with others, lest they judge him. Have you ever kept a secret for the same reason?

7. Josiah tries to be an encouragement to his brother, but can't seem to break through his barriers. Do you have a sibling you can talk openly with?

8. Sammy understands the need for secrecy and is a friend to many. Do you have a secret keeper you can trust?

9. When Jaden shares his struggles with Sammy, the older man gives him sometimes-tough, honest answers. Do you prefer straightforward answers or would you rather have answers be sugar-coated?

10. God works out everything for good for the characters in this book. Have you ever seen God turn one of your messes into a message?

A SPECIAL THANK YOU

Thank you to star reader **Sandy Seals**, who suggested the name Titus. His book is next in line!

I'd like to take this time to thank everyone that had any involvement in this book and its production, including my Mom and Dad, who have always been supportive of my writing, my longsuffering Family—especially my handsome, encouraging Hubby, my Amish and former-Amish friends who have helped immensely in my understanding of the Amish ways, my supportive Pastor and Church family, my Proofreaders, my Editor, my CIA Facebook author friends who have been a tremendous help, my wonderful Readers who buy, read, offer great input, and leave encouraging reviews and emails, my awesome Launch Team who, I'm confident, will 'Sprede the Word' about *The Teacher*! And last, but certainly not least, I'd like to thank my *Precious LORD and SAVIOUR JESUS CHRIST*, for without Him, none of this would have been possible!

If you haven't joined my Facebook reader group,
you may do so here:
https://www.facebook.com/groups/379193966104149/

Made in United States
Troutdale, OR
08/20/2024

22184656R00141